Andy Shepherd

THE BOY WHO SANG WITH DRAGONS

Illustrated by
Sara Ogilvie

Piccadilly
PRESS

First published in Great Britain in 2021 by
PICCADILLY PRESS
80-81 Wimpole Street, London W1G 9RE
Owned by Bonnier Books
Sveavägen 56, Stockholm, Sweden
www.piccadillypress.co.uk

ISBN: 978-1-84812-942-9
Also available as an ebook and in audio

1

Designed by Sue Michniewicz
Printed and bound in Great Britain by Clays Ltd, Elcograf S.p.A.

Piccadilly Press is an imprint of Bonnier Books UK
www.bonnierbooks.co.uk

For Ian, Ben and Jonas,
for helping me grow our dragons

Here in Grandad's garden, the air crackles
with magic. In between the runner beans
and raspberry bushes, dragons flit.
Scales shimmering. Eyes glittering.
Hot breath steaming.

I stand, feet rooted in the soil like a
plant. Growing tall and strong as tiny dragons
settle on my hands, my arms, my head.

An orange dragon with silver-tipped wings brushes
my face. A turquoise dragon with black spines and a
bright yellow tail scratches my palm. An electric-blue
dragon with threads of silver clings to my back.

And when I tilt my head upwards to the stars and close my eyes, I see the shining ruby shape of Flicker, huge and bright like a glowing constellation come to life.

Here in Grandad's garden, I am the dragon whisperer. The dragon protector.

1
Super-Sticky Slimo

'Incoming slime,' Ted yelled. And we all ducked as a green and brown-speckled dragon dived at us.

A splat of sticky goo landed on Liam's head.

'Eww! This stuff stinks,' he groaned. 'I thought only slugs oozed slime.'

'It's probably a defence mechanism,' Aura said. 'It must be scared.'

'Yeah, like hagfish,' Ted piped up, a bit too gleefully. 'They can squirt out a litre of slime if they feel threatened.'

'Well, this dragon must be terrified,' Liam said.

'We're going to be wading through the stuff soon.'

'You couldn't wade through this,' Kat said. 'It's super-sticky.' She waved her hands at us – they were covered in fluff from her efforts to wipe them clean.

'I think it's us who should be scared anyway,' Kai pointed out. 'Have you seen what those others are doing now?'

Two dragons with dainty feathery frills protruding from their elegant necks were hopping in circles in front of each other. Their heads bobbed and their frills fanned out, like those birds of paradise doing elaborate dances that I'd seen on TV.

'I think they're the least of our worries,' I said.

'Not those,' he said. '*Those*.' And he pointed to a pair of golden dragons with long curled horns and strange corkscrew-shaped tails. 'They're drilling holes in the cricket pitch!'

'And scorching the grass,' said Kat.

'And leaving muddy mounds like molehills,' said Ted.

An area of the neatly manicured pitch suddenly ignited.

'And then there's the explosive poo of course,' I added.

This particular band of dragons were certainly proving to be more of a handful than most of those who ventured out of Grandad's garden.

'We're not going to be able to see them soon,' Liam said. 'Let alone catch them.'

He was right – it was almost dark.

'Can you give us a bit of light?' I whispered to Zing, who was resting his head over my shoulder, claws digging into my jumper and tail swishing back and forth.

His sky-blue scales flared brightly and the tip of his zigzag tail pulsed white as it flicked out. A crackle of little blue sparks leaped from spike to spike along his back. I felt my hair starting to stick up, as a familiar buzz ran through me. Then he rose into the air.

He flew up and landed on one of the floodlights that lined the edge of the cricket pitch. The bulb blazed into life, illuminating the grass and the drilling dragons. I thought for a minute that might be enough to make them all fly off into the night. But no.

You've got to love my optimism, haven't you? You'd think I'd know better by now. Because let's face it, life with dragons is *never* easy.

As the light came on, the two dancing dragons started twisting and twirling even more wildly, as if this was the spotlight their dramatic display had been waiting for. But it was too alarming for the slime-

splattering dragon, which dripped its way over the top of the drilling dragons and then disappeared into one of the holes they'd made.

The next second it shot out of another hole a few feet away.

'They really have been burrowing,' I said. 'They must have made tunnels under there.'

The drilling dragons really didn't like their hard work being invaded. But Slimo was too quick for them. We watched as he dodged them and disappeared back down yet another hole.

'We need to do something,' Kat said. 'Or this cricket pitch is going to be more full of holes than a piece of Swiss cheese!'

'Everyone, stand guard over a hole,' I said. 'Get ready to grab hold of it next time it pops out.'

Now if you've ever played that game 'whack-a-mole' at school fetes where you have to whack a sock full of newspaper as it drops out the end of a pipe, you'll know that this was not as easy as it sounded.

Especially when the 'sock' in question was covered in slime and had wings and sharp claws!

It wasn't helped by the twirling dragons getting in on the action. They slalomed their way between us, getting closer and closer to our heads, as if they were in a competition to see which of them could make us flail about the most. The smaller one won, by sending Liam lurching backwards. He stumbled over one of the heaps of dirt they'd made and landed bottom first in a hole. Which was undignified enough, except then the hole collapsed into the tunnel underneath and he was left wedged into the ground, his arms and legs sticking up in the air.

'Help!' he wailed.

Kai hurried over and started trying to pull him out. I could see he was stifling a giggle. Liam looked less amused.

'Sorry, but you look like a hermit crab,' Kai said, as he managed to pull him out a few inches, only to give up and let go.

He turned to the rest of us. 'It's no good, I need a hand,' he called.

Kat joined in pulling Liam's other arm. And Aura and I each grabbed a leg.

'*And they pulled and heaved and yanked and tugged, but still the enormous turnip would not move,*' Kai chanted, and the stifled giggle finally burst out and infected us all.

'Ha ha!' Liam said crossly. He shook us all off and started wriggling, arms and legs all squished together and waving madly, making him look like an irate squid. Which just made us laugh even more.

It also had a strange effect on the slime in the tunnel.

'Er, guys,' Ted said. 'I think the suction from Liam's bum is causing a reaction.'

We all turned and looked. And to our horror we saw that coming out of the hole at the other end of the tunnel was a super-stretched slime bubble. And it was growing bigger by the second. Snot bubbles had nothing on this monstrosity.

2
Cake, Presents and a Jammy Dragon

So there are a few skills you definitely need if you want to grow dragons.

1. The ability to keep your eyes wide open. Including the extra pair of eyes you'll need to grow in the back of your head. They're essential for watching over the sneakier types.

2. Great listening skills. Sometimes, however wide your eyes are, it's only the fizzling, sizzling, steaming, scratching and general crashing of household items that will give them away.

3. Awesomely fast reflexes. For leaping to put out sparks, catching your aunt's priceless porcelain leopard on a log as it's sent flying off a shelf or jumping in front of your dragon and yelling, 'Giant diving dingbat!' while pointing at the sky – a useful technique to distract your nosy

neighbour from the truth: that it wasn't a fox
that upended his dustbin; it was your friendly,
but far too inquisitive, dragon.

4. Thinking on your feet. I'm telling you
now, however lively your imagination is
I can guarantee you won't predict every
scenario your dragon will land you in.
I mean, who would have thought of
giant slime bubbles, right?

5. Speaking of which, I should add a new
skill to the list. The ability to extract your
friend from a sticky slime capsule while
wrestling two startled corkscrew-tail dragons
and dodging the diving antics of a couple of
whirling, prancing 'look at me' type dragons.

By the time we'd safely caught all of the little visitors,
done our best to patch up the cricket pitch and returned

the dragons to Grandad's garden, where they could follow their recently hatched companions up into the sky and towards the shining North Star, we were all in need of the chocolate-fudge cake I'd brought along, thanks to Nana.

'I'm going to miss this,' Kat said.

'Me too,' said Ted, eyeing up the last couple of slices of cake.

'I don't think she means the cake,' I said, watching as Kat raised a hand. Rosebud unfurled her wings and detached herself from Aura's arm, where she'd been happily curled up throughout the afternoon's adventures. The little dragon fluttered over and landed on Kat's shoulder.

'You're not the only one,' Kai muttered.

Over the past few weeks the twins had been caught up in the excitement of visiting relatives and packing up their lives ready for their new adventure in China. But sitting now in their empty bedroom, the reality of their departure was getting hard to miss.

Ted looked a bit sheepish, although he still kept an eye on the remaining cake.

'I really hoped Crystal would visit before we left,' Kat said sadly.

Ever since the night our dragons had nearly been spotted flying over the village hall, and Kat had urged them to stay away for a while, there had been no sign of them.

Until then, even though we hadn't ever known when they might turn up, we knew they would come back to us eventually. But despite watching and waiting from our windows every night, and desperately hoping, not one of them had returned.

I kept telling myself that Flicker would come back, of course he would. But there was a nagging doubt that burrowed its way deep inside me. And the longer the sky remained empty, the more settled that doubt had become. It'd be redecorating before long, repainting my insides in shades of queasy yellow Fear and sickly green Uncertainty.

I looked up to find the whole superhero squad lost in thought. Their faces were equally gloomy.

I leaped to my feet, determined to change the mood, and managed to startle Aura so much she flung out her hand, sending her last piece of cake hurtling past her mouth and into Ted's forehead.

'Waste not want not,' he said, wiping it off and quickly shoving the cake into his mouth before Aura could object. I could have told him she was unlikely to want to eat anything that had been stuck to his face, but he obviously felt differently.

'I've got something that'll cheer you up,' I said. 'We all have, haven't we?'

'Absolutely!' Aura grinned. 'Can I give them my present first?' And she started rummaging in her bag.

Kat and Kai perked up at the mention of 'presents'.

'Here it is,' she said at last, waving a crumpled piece of paper triumphantly. She handed it to Kat.

Kat looked at it. 'This is brilliant,' she said, grinning. 'Thanks, Aura.'

'Yeah, thanks,' echoed Kai. 'You've really done your homework. This is going to be so much fun to do.'

Seeing my confusion, Kat passed me the piece of paper. It read: 'Kat and Kai's Treasure Trail'. And it was a list of places to visit and things to spot once they arrived in China, with a box to tick next to each one. It went all the way from 'airport snacks' to the last item on the list, which was: 'dragon fruit'.

I laughed. 'You'd better keep your eyes open then!'

I had to hand it to Aura – it was a great idea. And it would be the perfect accompaniment to the present I had for them.

'Me next,' Ted said. And he produced a drawstring sack stuffed with chocolate bars and biscuits and even some jam tarts. 'In case you get homesick.' He grinned.

'Yum!' Kai said, and fished out a bar of chocolate. He passed the sack to Kat who peered in, and promptly pulled out an empty wrapper. She raised her eyes at Ted, who cleared his throat awkwardly.

'It's a perfect present, Ted,' she said, laughing. 'Thanks.'

Liam gave them his presents next. First there was

one of his favourite comics for Kat. Which got a serious nod of approval from both Kat and me. We knew how hard it was to give up a well-loved comic. And for Kai a key ring in the shape of a dragon's eye that had a fierce little torch in it, making the eye shine.

It was almost my turn. But first: 'This is from Lolli,' I said. I handed them a rolled-up piece of paper. On it

Lolli had painted a picture of Kat and Kai with Crystal and Dodger.

'Er . . . Is that jam?' Kai said holding the picture up to his face and tentatively sniffing it.

I grinned. ''Fraid so.'

'Tell her we love it,' Kat said, her eyes sparkling as she stared at the jammy dragons.

'And these are from me,' I said. I pulled two scrapbooks out of my bag.

There was a little 'ooh' from Aura when she saw them. And nods from Liam and Ted. Kat and Kai went a bit quiet. I'd decorated the covers with loads of photos of us all. I'd spent ages cutting and sticking them on and shaping them into the outline of a dragon.

'I thought you could put pictures inside and write about stuff that happens,' I said. 'So you can keep a record. You know, like Elvi did. And then when you come back you can show us all your amazing adventures.'

Kat gave a little squeak and pulled me into a

massive hug. And then I noticed that Kai was rubbing his eye as if Zing had flicked a raisin into it.

'We are part of the best superhero squad ever. Fact,' he said.

I grinned. He was right, we were.

3
A Waggle, a Wave and a Little Wise Piglet

'So, Chipstick,' said Grandad. 'Did they like their presents?'

I nodded.

'What time they off then?'

I knocked a clod of mud off the hoe I was holding, hoping it would cover the wobble in my voice.

'They've already gone. They had to leave for the airport at five o'clock this morning.'

Grandad dug his spade into the ground and took a deep breath of the chilly morning air. He glanced at his watch and then up at the sky.

'Two hours to get to the airport, two hours to check in, an hour to board.' He counted out the timings on his fingers and then paused. 'Hey up, that'll be them now.'

He pointed to the sky, at the smoky trail of an aeroplane passing overhead.

He started jumping up and down and waving madly.

'Come on then, Chipstick, give them a wave. We need to give them a proper send-off.'

I shook my head and laughed. And we spent the next few minutes doing our farewell wave routine, now with added leaps, bottom waggling and arm spinning. We were soon both out of breath and collapsed into each other in giggles. The chances of Kat and Kai being on that plane were probably a gazillion to one, but I imagined their grinning faces at the little round windows anyway.

'The world's not as big as you think,' Grandad whispered. 'None of us is as far apart as all that.'

After refuelling with a jam tart and a mug of milk in Grandad's shed, we got back to the digging and hoeing.

I cleared the ground around the dragon-fruit tree, pulling out a nettle that had shot up and a few straggly weeds, but leaving the last few dandelions of the year, because Grandad insisted they were good for the bees.

Underneath the nettle a funny little shoot was poking out of the ground. My heart gave a flutter. Was it a dragon-fruit seedling?

I crouched down and peered at it, and then realised the two little leaves were the wrong shape.

I should have known really. After all, we'd never found any growing in Grandad's garden. It was too cold for them. It was why the seedlings from the botanic garden were so important. Except now all the ones we'd collected and had been looking after had died. The only others were locked away in a greenhouse in the botanic garden, under the care of Chouko, the botanist and gardener who worked there.

Those seedlings had looked strong and healthy. And I still didn't know what it was that she was doing differently. How was she succeeding in growing them, when I'd failed so miserably?

'I reckon they'll be better off over at mine,' said a voice from the other side of the tree. 'More room, and I can keep my eye on them.'

'Oh, I expect they'll be all right in there. They've done OK so far,' Grandad said.

I stepped out and saw Jim, Grandad's neighbour – the man I used to call Grim, that is until I took a leaf out of Grandad's book. Grandad always says, 'Find the kind, and you never know what else you'll find.' And he was right. The day I stopped seeing Jim as the enemy, he . . . well, he stopped being the enemy. I found out he wasn't so bad after all. In fact, if it hadn't been for him, my head might not have caught up with my heart enough to know I had to let Flicker go.

Of course, he could still be a bit rough around the edges, so sometimes I had to remind myself to be nice to him in response to any grumpiness. As I watched, he strode over the little fence between the gardens, a tray tucked under his arm.

'No, no. Let's not take any chances,' he continued. 'It's an honour to be chosen to grow the flowers for the centrepiece of the Village in Bloom show. We can't mess about with that. I've bought a new polytunnel – just the ticket for hothousing these beauties. And I'll be back later to pick up the willow arch too.'

He gave me a brief nod hello and then headed into Grandad's greenhouse and started loading his tray up with pots, leaving Grandad scratching his beard.

'What's he doing?' I asked.

Grandad's eyes twinkled as he smiled down at me. 'Oh, you know Jim. He's got a plan in his head, that's all. Just sometimes he forgets we're supposed to be doing this project together.'

'But you've been working really hard at looking after all of those flowers. You shouldn't let him just take everything over to his.'

'It's OK. No doubt he's right. They'll be better off in that polytunnel of his.'

I must have frowned, because Grandad nudged me. 'He might not go about it in the best way, but he's only trying to do the right thing for the show. We're a team. He knows that, even if he doesn't always show it. I wouldn't want to be doing all this work on my own, that's for sure. And I don't suppose he would either. A lot of responsibility for one person.'

'I guess so,' I said.

'I know so,' said Grandad. 'Things are always friendlier with two. Someone clever said that once.'

'Who?' I asked.

'A very small piglet. Friend to a very wise bear.'

4
Are We Growing Choclit Now?

My sister Lolli skips everywhere, and not gentle skipping. She's a fierce skipper. The trouble is, sometimes the momentum is so forceful she ends up going *splat* on her face. Which is exactly what I saw her do as she skipped after Aura who was coming through the fruit trees towards me. I winced at the sight of Lolli sprawled on the ground.

Hearing the little yelp behind her, Aura turned. She hurried back and lifted Lolli up, dusting down her tutu, straightening her Batman cape and popping her star-shaped sunglasses back on.

Undaunted, Lolli launched back into skipping, but at least with Aura holding her hand, this time she made it up the garden in one piece.

'You know, if you wore trousers, you'd be able to see your feet,' I teased as Lolli raced up and hugged me.

'A shorter cape might help too,' added Aura.

'But trousers aren't twirly,' she said, unpeeling herself and spinning round. 'And Batman *always* wears his cape.'

'It is pretty twirly,' Aura said with a laugh as the cape swung out.

'You need capes and tutus too,' Lolli said. 'Then we can all go twirly.'

I grinned and, holding her tightly, we spun round and round, faster and faster until Lolli's feet flew off the ground and I almost staggered into the spiky leaves of the dragon-fruit tree.

Eventually I put her down and, still giggling, she scampered over to Grandad.

'Where's the choclit, Guppie? Nana said you putting choclit on the garden. But *I* want some.'

She looked around at the vegetable plot and peered into the wheelbarrow. Then she turned to me, looking rather cross.

'Did you eat it all, Tomas?'

I laughed, but then realised by the stern look she gave me that she really wasn't joking.

Her lip suddenly wobbled. 'That's not fair,' she said.

I glanced at Grandad, confused.

He smiled and wrapped an arm around Lolli. 'I'm sorry, Lolli, I think you might have got the wrong end of the stick,' he said gently.

She sniffed the air. 'But I can smell choclit. And anyway, all my sticks are home in bed, even sticky Herbert cos he's hurt his head again.'

Grandad chortled. 'I've been spreading cocoa mulch. It's made from the shells of cocoa beans. That's what chocolate is made from,' he explained when she still looked blankly at him. 'That's what you can smell.'

'So there's no yummy choclit bars?'

He shook his head sadly.

'It's great for the garden though,' he added happily. 'Keeps down the weeds, gives the soil food and nutrients when it breaks down, and the worms love it too!'

I knew that Lolli, who had an imagination as fantastically fizzy as mine, had probably been picturing chocolate bars hanging like bean pods ripe for the picking.

Poor Lollibob!

I fished around in my pocket, but only found the remains of a marshmallow stuck in there.

'Here you go,' Aura said. And she handed Lolli a little chocolate frog. 'He's been living in a pocket so he might be a bit melty,' she added apologetically.

Lolli gave a wobbly smile. 'I love him,' she said, then hugged Aura quickly before tearing the wrapper open and popping the frog in her mouth.

'Thanks,' I whispered.

As usual Grandad was right. Doing things together *was* friendlier. Even picking slugs off plants and carting barrows of cocoa mulch around was more fun with Aura. She was a bit like Ted throwing out facts, except with her it was all about dragons and often about the stories she'd grown up reading. Like me, *The Reluctant Dragon* was one of her favourites. But she knew loads of other books I'd never even heard of. I needed another trip to see Mrs Olive at the library to check them all out.

At last, with aching arms, we collapsed on the bench outside the shed.

Rosebud was flitting around the garden, landing on plants and bushes and then fluttering off again, as if she was inspecting them. And Zing was darting between the branches of an apple tree, letting out little sizzling lightning bolts that left jagged scorch marks on the fruit. Aura watched them, a big contented smile on her face.

'You really are lucky, Tomas,' she said. 'This place is completely brilliant. And now with added chocolate!'

I laughed. 'Yeah, it's a shame we can't actually grow chocolate bars. Just as well we grow dragons to make up for it!'

Aura nodded and grinned. 'I don't know why,' she said, 'but I just get this lovely feeling whenever I walk through your nana's kitchen. And then you come out here and –' she waved her hand at the garden – 'there's all this, just waiting. Like the best-kept secret.'

5
Lights, Camera, Mayhem!

My house is usually pretty busy, what with Dad working from home, Lolli on the loose and Mum offering a place to stay to every stray animal she comes across. But when I got home on Monday, with Aura in tow, we found a whole new level of crazy even for us.

Five people with cameras and clipboards and one waving a brush in my mum's face were crammed into the lounge. Along with a Shetland pony, a chatty cockatoo, a large vivarium full of snakes, a hastily put-together enclosure for a gang of gerbils and a furious-looking Tomtom. Everyone was rushing around, tripping over wires, adjusting lights, moving furniture and talking at about a thousand miles an hour to each other.

We squeezed past a man wearing a bright orange turban and even brighter orange trainers who was talking excitedly on his phone. Without a pause, he grinned and gave us a thumbs up.

'What on earth is going on, Mum?'

'Oh, Tomas,' she cried above the din of the animals and the chatter of people. 'The radio show has been spotted by a TV producer. We're making a live show! Isn't it brilliant?!'

I looked at Aura, who was watching my dad chasing a gerbil, while another one climbed up his trouser leg. 'I don't think cardboard was the best idea for a gerbil enclosure,' she whispered.

Mum waved. 'There are oat-and-raisin cookies over there – help yourself.' She might have been about to say something else, but the cockatoo flew at her head and she had to divert.

'Shall we grab some cookies then?' Aura said. I

watched the man with the make-up brush, who'd failed to get any powder anywhere near Mum, holding a half-bitten cookie. The look on his face was one I recognised from a life-time of eating my mum's desserts.

'Best not,' I said. And motioned to the man, who was now discreetly crumbling the cookie into the gerbil enclosure. Which felt a bit mean to the gerbils, if you ask me. Still, at least with all the holes they'd nibbled in the cardboard, they had an escape plan.

'I'm so glad you're back,' Dad said, passing us a gerbil each. 'Can you try and contain these lot while I look for Mr Floppybobbington? Lolli's at Bea's house and I'm supposed to be on bunny watch. Only it's all got a bit out of hand.'

'Of course,' I said. 'We just need to pop upstairs.'

Helping wasn't a problem, but helping while you had a dragon tucked into your clothes was less easy.

'No time, Tomas,' Dad squeaked. 'We go live in five.'

So you know when you watch something live on TV and things go a bit wrong and the presenters all get a bit giggly. Well, just imagine a small living room, a LOT of animals, one presenter who looks terrified of anything with teeth, my mum with a cockatoo permanently attached to her head and a rebel stunt gerbil who decides to launch himself at the woman filming it all. Oh, and then add in a dragon who keeps farting green giggle gas. That's some serious live TV right there.

At least Zing getting fidgety in my coat and charging up like a battery – and then unleashing an electric shock that fried the camera – stopped the live broadcast before Tomtom tore the hairy microphone to shreds and the presenter slipped and fell bottom first in the Shetland pony poo.

'That's a wrap,' the man in the orange turban said.

He gave Mum a thumbs up. 'Same time next week, then?'

While the TV crew dismantled all the equipment and loaded it back into their van we slumped on the sofa.

'I'm sure it'll get easier,' I said.

'Absolutely,' said Dad, giving Mum a squeeze and rescuing the gerbil nesting in her hair.

Mum smiled, then jumped when the doorbell rang. 'Oh dear, they're not back already, are they?'

'I think that'll be Mamma, come to pick me up,' Aura said. 'She wanted to say hi and meet everyone. I hope that's OK?'

Mum looked around at the mess. 'Absolutely. Probably best she gets to see the real us, don't you agree, Tomas?'

Aura's mum didn't bat an eyelid when she came in. In fact she was so captivated by the cockatoo on my mum's head that Dad had to gently point out the pony poo she was just about to step in.

'It's so lovely to finally meet you all,' she said, reaching out to shake hands with Mum and Dad. 'I'm

Rosa.' She was wearing a pair of denim dungarees, red boots covered in flowers and a bright yellow scarf. She had the same beaming smile as her daughter, and we couldn't resist beaming right back.

'Tomas,' she said. 'I've heard so much about you.'

I shook her hand and grinned an apology as the pony started nudging her leg.

'Expect she can smell this,' she laughed, and fished out an apple from her pocket. 'Is it OK to give it to her?' she asked. Mum nodded and Rosa offered it to the now-delighted pony.

By the time Liam and Bea's mum dropped Lolli off half an hour later, it felt as if I'd known Rosa forever. And Lolli obviously felt that same familiarity. She immediately settled herself on Rosa's lap and started recounting her afternoon, in between licks of a sticky and slightly hairy lollipop.

6
Soaring to the Stars

Every night after Mum had kissed me goodnight and Dad had done his 'rock 'n' roll' tuck-in, I wriggled back out of bed and opened the window to peer out at the night sky. I scanned the clouds, keeping my eyes wide open, desperately hoping I'd see a glimmer of red. But tonight, just like every evening since the dragons had been told to keep a low profile, it looked as if Flicker would only be visiting me in my dreams.

I kept the window ajar in case Zing wanted to explore, and climbed back into bed. But the little dragon left the windowsill where he'd been scratching at the wood and darted over to me. Recently he'd found a new favourite game, flying from one end of my bed to the other, seeing how low he could skim over me without bashing into me. To be fair he flew with a lot more control than he had in the past. But even so, the amount of times I got hit in the face by a wing or scratched by a claw meant I still wasn't sure this was *my* favourite game.

I rolled over and stuck a pillow on my head for protection, at least that would catch any stray wing tips or claws. Then I drifted off to sleep with Zing whizzing back and forth above me.

I woke up feeling as if something was wrong. Like there was something I was really worried about only I didn't know what it was. I rubbed my eyes and stared around the dim room. Zing had finally fallen asleep at the bottom of my bed. He was stretched out, wings lying across my feet and his body tucked in the gap between.

A little puff of cloud floated in through the window. I rubbed my eyes harder as it hovered in front of me and I saw little sparks dancing inside it. When I heard a low rumble I leaped out of bed, sending a startled and still dozy Zing flapping into the air.

I rushed to the window and flung it open, my whole body buzzing and crackling with energy. In fact, if I'd had silver threads like Zing they'd have been flashing like lightning across my body. I stared out into Flicker's diamond eyes.

'I knew you'd come back!' I cried. 'I knew it!' Though given the huge electric current of relief I'd felt seeing his eyes twinkle back at me, I had to admit there had been a secret part of me that was worried I might never see him again.

As Zing zipped out of the window and perched on Flicker's horn, I clambered onto the sill and stretched one leg over his back.

'There's someone I really want you to meet,' I whispered.

Of course Aura had seen lots of little dragons since she'd first met Zing and Rosebud. And I'd told her all about Flicker. Endlessly, in fact. But the truth is, you can't do a dragon like Flicker justice in words.

I wanted Aura to meet him for herself.

As we went soaring over the village, Zing clung to Flicker's horn, obviously content to hitch a ride. I stretched out my arms as if they were wings and a whoop of happiness bubbled out of me. Flicker's scales shimmered red to gold as we flew on.

I whispered directions into his ear and Flicker rumbled again and blew out another puff of breath that crackled with sparks.

As we circled the park I spotted two familiar shapes in the sky ahead. I waved and called out to Liam and Ted, who were riding Maxi and Sunny in formation, wing tip to wing tip. I hoped that somewhere far across the world, Crystal and Dodger had found Kat and Kai too.

Leaving the others to race, I pointed downward and Flicker flew lower, blowing a cloud of smoke that hung like mist and camouflaged us from any nosy neighbours. When we reached Aura's house Flicker leaned his head against the little balcony outside her window. I scrambled off, careful not to send any of the flowers and pots crashing to the floor. Luckily she always left the window ajar for Rosebud. I leaned in and hissed her name.

She didn't stir, but a bud next to me unfurled and a sleepy Rosebud lifted her head and stared up at Flicker and Zing.

'Aura,' I tried again. Still nothing. Zing flew down from Flicker's horn and through the gap. He rocketed across the room and landed with a bump on Aura's bed, then started clawing at her sheet. He was obviously as eager to get back out into the star-speckled night as I was.

45

Even the heaviest sleeper would have trouble sleeping through a dragon tearing at their bed, especially one whose tail kept thumping on their forehead.

Aura sprang up in alarm as if she was being attacked – which she kind of was.

Her eyes flew from Zing to me, leaning in through the window.

'Tomas, what on earth are you . . .' she hissed. And then her final word 'you' disappeared in an awestruck gasp, as she spotted Flicker's giant head outside.

'I wanted to introduce you to someone,' I said, grinning. 'Hurry up!'

Aura didn't breathe a word as she looked into Flicker's eyes and then followed me as I clambered onto his back. But I guess even the most talkative person is likely to feel a bit tongue-tied the first time they climb onto a dragon.

With Rosebud nestled in Aura's dressing gown and Zing now clinging to my back, Flicker rose up through the smoky mist, an almighty burst of glittering red

against the inky black of the sky. We began to swoop and dive and soar and after a few minutes I craned my head back to check that this unusually silent Aura was OK. The beaming grin and her bright twinkling eyes reassured me she was a lot more than OK.

But it was only when Flicker took us on a stomach-churning loop the loop that the squeal of delight finally came, as though Flicker had known that was what was needed for her to fully let go and enjoy the ride.

'I haven't got any words,' she whispered as we levelled off, our stomachs still floating somewhere among the stars.

I grinned. 'You don't need words for this.'

Grandad always says that some things live in places words don't reach. And dragons are most definitely one of them.

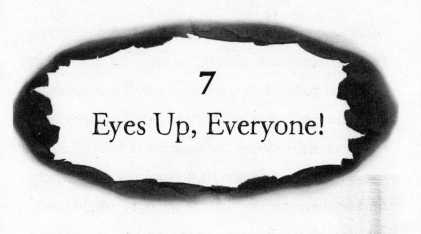

7
Eyes Up, Everyone!

As we soared home later, after dropping a beaming Aura back onto her balcony, I rested my face against Flicker's neck and wrapped my arms tightly around him.

'I've missed you,' I whispered.

Flicker's scales glimmered turquoise, and feeling the warmth from them, I let out a little sigh.

'At least I can tell Lolli you're back,' I said.

Tinkle rarely came at night with the other dragons, but if they felt safe to return, maybe I could promise Lolli that she too would see her dragon again at last. 'You will come again soon, won't you? And bring Tinkle?'

Flicker's wings beat slower. And just for a moment I saw the scales under my hands grow dull, their shine fading. And the rumble I felt against my cheek sounded more like a sigh than a contented purr. I squeezed him tighter, pushing away the same unsettled feeling I'd had on waking. I didn't want some unknown worry spoiling this moment.

Outside my window, Flicker dipped his head and I climbed down onto the sill. I stared into his eyes, where a rainbow of colours danced and dazzled.

Then I stood and watched as he rose up into the sky and disappeared amid the clouds.

The next day after school I headed with the rest of the superhero squad to the bus stop and together we took the short bus ride to the botanic garden. I'd begun to wonder if the unsettled feeling I'd had the night before was about the seedlings. They might be safe in

Chouko's hands for the time being, but it still wasn't a great idea to have anyone getting too close a look at them. Glancing around at the others, I was glad they'd all agreed to come too.

I'd also decided it was time to face Chouko. The last time Aura and I had seen her, her house had almost gone up in flames after Zing had got trapped in her greenhouse. And then we'd run off and left her to deal with the mess, too worried about the little dragon causing any more chaos. It was time to try and make amends, if she'd let us.

Everyone was full of the previous night's excitement, and the thrill of knowing the dragons had returned. We'd all received a full-capitals text from Kat declaring: 'THEY'RE BACK! THEY FOUND US!'

But as I led everyone along the path through the trees towards the little gardener's cottage where Chouko lived, our chatter petered out. All of us were wondering what kind of reception we'd get.

As we walked past one of the benches that were dotted around the garden, I saw that someone had been having a picnic and had left their litter on the grass.

We chased the fluttering crisp packets and picked up the empty sandwich cartons and discarded bottles of water.

'Thank you for doing that,' a voice said behind us. 'I really don't understand people sometimes.'

I spun round and saw Chouko coming towards us. Immediately, all the guilt and worry I felt leaped onto my face and started pulling my mouth in all sorts of weird directions. What started as an attempt at a friendly smile got yanked into a look of horror. I should have taken a moment before we met to think about what I could possibly say to her. She held my gaze for a second and then slowly smiled. Either she'd chosen to forgive or had forgotten our last meeting.

'Perhaps people think we have fairies at the bottom of the garden who will tidy up after them,' she said.

'I don't know about fairies, but I know some dragons who'd give them a fiery reminder,' Liam muttered quietly.

'How is your little friend doing?' she asked. For one awful second I thought she meant Zing. 'I seem to remember you were having trouble with a cactus you were growing.'

I smiled, relieved that she hadn't spotted the little dragon that day and that I now had the perfect opportunity to ask about the dragon-fruit seedlings.

'Not too well actually,' I said. 'In fact I wanted to ask you about it. We noticed you had some similar-looking cacti growing in your greenhouse.'

Chouko glanced at Aura and I quickly continued before she got too caught up remembering our obviously not forgotten previous visit.

'I just wondered what you do to keep them looking so healthy.'

Chouko wrinkled her nose and gave a little shrug. 'Nothing particular,' she said. 'The usual – a little warmth, not too much water, plenty of light. Maybe it's all the stories I tell them about the gardens I've visited around the world.' She chuckled. 'You know, they do almost glow with good health.'

I silently hoped that this was just a figure of speech and they weren't actually glowing like the dragon fruits did before the dragons hatched. That really would attract attention.

'I'm on my way to look for some more if you'd like to join me?' she said. 'Ten eager eyes are surely better than two! So long as you keep to the path,' she added, giving me a friendly nudge.

We followed Chouko into the glasshouse and through to the area where I'd found the last seedling. We all started scanning the ground. But Chouko giggled. 'Eyes up, everyone,' she said.

Confused, I looked up to where she was pointing, to the tree above us with its glossy oval leaves.

'I found all the other seedlings up in this one's branches,' she said. 'They seem to just love this tree.

Some plants like to hide out in the canopy where it's safer.'

'No wonder you couldn't find any more,' Aura whispered. 'You must have collected all the ones on the ground, but who knew they could climb trees!'

'They must be epiphytes,' Ted said excitedly. 'That means organisms that grow on other plants and get what they need from the air and rain. They're usually pollinated by hummingbirds,' he added, and I had the feeling he was about to launch into full-on fact-file mode.

Chouko nodded, obviously impressed with Ted's knowledge.

I turned my gaze up and spotted a cluster of little seedlings, their tiny spiked

leaves reaching out in my direction. Chouko spotted them too and clapped her hands delightedly.

Then Liam called out, 'Over here.' And everyone looked to see where he was pointing. Chouko hurried over with her collecting tray and carefully started gathering up the ones he'd found.

'Well done,' she cried. 'Excellent spotting!'

I quickly untangled one of the little seedlings from the branch it was clinging to and popped it into my pocket before she returned.

8
A Bolt from the Blue

At Aura's house the next day, I cradled the little seedling in my hand and looked expectantly at her.

'Maybe you should have left it on the tree,' she said. 'Or let Chouko take it with her like the rest. I don't really know any more than you do about looking after them. At least they were thriving back in her greenhouse.'

I felt my shoulders sag. I'd reached out and taken the seedling without really thinking. And ever since, I'd questioned whether I'd done the right thing. All I wanted was to try again. Maybe if I told it stories it would glow for me too? After all, with my imagination I bet my stories could rival Chouko's. But hearing Aura's doubts made me less sure of myself.

I thought again of Elvi and Arturo, the two people who knew the most about the dragon-fruit tree, after finding the seeds in the Hidden Dragon City. Elvi had spent years looking after the tree in her garden, way back before it had become Grandad's. Her diaries, which we'd found under Grandad's shed, had already told us so much. But I knew there was more to find. For one thing, the missing letters from Arturo. If only we could find those, then maybe there would be something in them that could help. But despite a thorough search I'd still not managed to discover any more hiding places at Nana and Grandad's. At this point I was pretty much relying on Aura's green fingers to help me.

She took the seedling carefully from my hands and settled it into the pot of soil she'd got ready.

'Maybe Rosebud could use that breath of hers to keep it healthy,' I said hopefully.

'Maybe,' Aura agreed. 'Let's hope so anyway.'

We watched as Aura lifted Rosebud until her nose touched one of the seedling's leaves. The little dragon let out an orange breath. And then a fart too – filling the air with a sweet-smelling green gas.

'I don't suppose it'll suddenly start sprouting dragon fruits straight away,' Aura giggled as we both stared intently at it.

I snorted, the gas making my head swim and the laughter erupt out of me. Zing, who'd got a snout full of the green gas, had immediately revved up and was now crashing into the lampshade overhead, sending it rocking to and fro before he dived down and landed in a somersault on Aura's bed. By this time we were rolling about on the floor in uncontrollable hysterics.

Suddenly hearing footsteps on the stairs, Aura tucked Rosebud out of sight and I launched myself onto her bed, throwing a pillow onto a squirming Zing to hide him.

The door opened and Aura's mum popped her head in. Now that the effects of the green gas had passed, we were left, our faces streaming with tears of laughter, wondering what exactly had been quite so funny.

'Hello, Tomas.' She peered round the door. 'Just checking for ponies or gerbils. Or camera crews.' She gave me a grin – the kind of grin that made me think she might have just dropped a centipede down my back and was dying to burst out laughing and tell me.

'All OK in here then?'

'All fine, thanks, Mamma,' Aura said sweetly.

I nodded and started to smile, but the smile got lost

on its way up my face. Because right then something exploded in my head. And it wasn't dragon poo!

My brain had done the most monumental backflip and was standing proudly like an Olympic athlete who knows they've just won gold. And to be fair, this bolt of recognition really was gold-medal-worthy. It had happened at the exact moment that Aura's mum had given me that grin.

'Isn't that right, Tomas?' Aura said from somewhere far, far away. 'Tomas?'

I shook my head and then nodded fiercely when they looked confused. I added a manic double thumbs up and a wide-mouthed grinace to be on the safe side – (a grinace is actually a grimace you've forced to become a grin. They can be a bit scary at the best of times, but when you add in a dragon under your bum who might just set light to your pants, a grinace can be pretty terrifying to behold). Aura's mum backed out of the room warily, obviously deciding to leave us to it.

'What's up with you?' Aura hissed, still watching

the door. 'We're supposed to be flying under the radar, not drawing attention to ourselves. What's with the –' she waved her hand at me – 'face?' she finished.

I'm one of those people whose face pretty much acts out what's going on in my brain. I'm a bit of an open book that way. As I reached a hand up to my cheek, I realised my face must have been trying and failing to fathom what on earth had just happened.

You see, I had just had the biggest shock ever. And if you're wondering what on earth had got into me to make me act this way, just take a minute. Because the clues were all there. The truth had been right in front of me all along. Standing in front of me right now in fact.

Some of you might have figured this out already. And if you have, then a gazillion points to you; you definitely have your eyes open enough to look after dragons. But anyone who's looking as confused as Aura was, here's the thing. The thing I absolutely needed to tell my friend. And here's how I did it.

9
When the Clouds Clear

The very first thing I did was leap off her bed and race over to her computer, where I started jabbing at the keyboard.

'Just give me a sec,' I said. 'I need to be absolutely sure about this.'

As soon as the words came up on the screen, I let out a little squeak and the breath I'd been holding.

I sat there for a second, my brain whizzing and fizzing.

'I think I know why you feel so at home at my nana and grandad's,' I blurted at last.

Aura looked at me, curiosity etching tiny lines on her forehead and making her nose wrinkle.

I had the distinct feeling she thought my recent behaviour was a bit of an over-reaction for this simple statement.

'Well, the combination of your nana's cooking and a dragon-fruit tree is pretty hard to beat, I guess.'

'It's not just that,' I said quickly. 'It's your mum.'

'Mamma?'

'Her name's Rosa?'

'Yeah. That's why I called this one Rosebud,' she said, cradling her little dragon's head in her hand.

'And your grandma . . . you called her "Amma", right?'

'Yes. But that's not her name. It's just like grandma, but in –'

'Icelandic. I know,' I said, finishing the sentence before she could.

'That's right,' Aura said sounding surprised and just a bit impressed. 'Not many people know that.'

'I didn't either. That's what I just looked up,' I said, waving at the computer.

'Look, what's going on, Tomas?'

'Your amma was from Iceland,' I went on. 'But she travelled all over the world. And she ended up . . .' I paused, 'here.'

Aura looked confused. 'In this little village, yeah. But so what?'

Aura was looking utterly bewildered. But I'm guessing your brain has caught right up!

'Your amma's name was Elvi, wasn't it?' I said.

Aura looked utterly flummoxed now.

'The reason you feel so at home in my nana and grandad's house is because I'm pretty sure you've been there before. With Elvi.'

Aura still looked blank. I'd need to spell this out even clearer.

'She lived there, Aura. It was her garden.'

'That's crazy,' Aura said. 'I'd know if I'd been there before.'

'Not if you were really little. Anyway, I think perhaps you remember deep down. You told me about sloes growing there. You said yourself you didn't know how you even knew what a sloe was. And you've always said how the kitchen felt friendly. I think that's because it was already familiar.'

Aura stared at me. Expressions swept across her face like clouds speeding across the sky. Confusion, disbelief and suspicion that I was somehow teasing, which led to a pretty stormy cloud of irritation.

'It's true,' I said softly.

'I don't know, Tomas,' she said after a minute. 'I really don't remember it. I think you must have made a mistake.'

'I haven't. I'm positive,' I said. 'And I can prove

it.' I pictured the photo I'd found when I first discovered Elvi had known about the dragons. 'Your amma had a small tattoo of a dragon on her wrist, didn't she?'

Aura nodded slowly.

'I know Elvi,' I said. And then I added quietly, 'I have her diaries.'

On the way to Grandad's garden I described the photo of Elvi standing in front of a wall from the Hidden City, with the exact same grin Aura's mum had just flashed at me. Then I breathlessly rattled off the full story about finding the dragon-fruit tree, the encyclopedia in Grandad's shed with Elvi's name and discovering all the letters and photos. And finally I told her about the photo I'd found later of Elvi holding a little baby and the words 'Sweet Rosa, 1979'. Aura's eyes went wide at hearing all about this.

I was sure if she could only stand in the garden again, she would remember.

Red-faced and panting, we raced down the garden path, sending Nana and Grandad a wave through the kitchen window.

We careered to a stop and I waited – jiggling like an expectant Lolli – waiting for the penny to well and truly drop.

There was a moment of quiet while the garden seemed to hold its breath around us. Like it too was waiting for her to remember.

I wasn't sure if I should say anything – she'd gone into a little trance and was just staring at a bunch of red stalks sprouting out of the ground. But after a while she raised her hand, finger pointing at the stalks. Then she suddenly started jabbing her finger at them wildly.

I watched as in that instant all the clouds cleared and Aura's face lit up with the sunny glow of the truth.

'Dogwood,' she cried. 'There were huge bushes of red dogwood.' She spun round. 'And there were more beehives than there are now. And two sheds, not just that one. And . . . and . . . we picked elderflowers from that tree and made cordial in the summer, and I had raspberry sorbet that stained my shorts. And we picked peas that I ate from the pods.'

Aura grabbed my arms and jumped up and down in front of me. 'I remember it, Tomas. All of it.'

Laughing now, she dragged me around the garden recounting all the details that had come flooding back into her mind.

Eventually she stopped in front of the dragon-fruit tree. We both looked at the spiky cactus leaves. I don't know why, but just for a split second I didn't want to ask if she remembered the tree. Or the dragons.

'I've always thought I was remembering stories,' she said quietly. 'Amma's stories. But the dragons were real all along.' She paused and looked at me.

'We grew dragons!'

10
A Blurt and a Blunder

'That's incredible,' said Ted later, when he and Liam came over.

'Amazing,' agreed Liam.

I nodded and stuffed another handful of popcorn into my mouth while they wrapped their heads around the news that Aura was Elvi's granddaughter.

'So she remembers the dragons?'

I nodded again. 'She does now. It all came back to her in a rush once we were back in the garden.'

'But Arturo's not her grandad?' Ted asked.

'No. I wondered about that too. But her grandfather's name was Miguel.'

'Maybe Elvi met him through Arturo when she visited him in Mexico?'

I shrugged. 'Maybe.'

'Had Aura heard of Arturo?' Ted asked.

I shook my head.

'Bit of a head-spinner for you, Tomas,' Liam said.

'For us all, I'd say,' Ted pointed out, reaching for another chocolate biscuit.

'Yeah, but especially Tomas. I mean he's always been Grand High DragonMaster. Maybe we should start calling Aura "Queen of the Dragons", like she always wanted.'

'Queen of the Dragons,' I whispered.

My hand clutching the popcorn went limp and little kernels of puffed corn rained down onto the carpet like tiny fluffy clouds.

Ted dug Liam in the ribs and laughed awkwardly.

'Come on,' he said, jumping to his feet and pulling me along with him. 'Let's go and raid the kitchen for some more of those biscuits, hey, Tomas?'

The next day on the way to school, Aura came racing up to me, her hair looking even more messy than usual.

'Tomas,' she hissed, 'we need to talk.' And she dragged me out of the way of Kayin and her mum, who was wrestling a double buggy past some wheelie bins that were blocking the pavement.

'What is it?' I asked. 'Is Rosebud OK?' I glanced upwards and then peered into Aura's jacket. She shook me off. 'She's at home, she's fine. It's nothing like that. It's Mamma.'

I must have looked even more alarmed, but she waved it away.

'She's fine too. Well, sort of. Oh, I don't know. Is

someone fine if they can't see what's right in front of them?'

I stared blankly at her. I was used to Aura talking fast, but right now it was like the words were in an Olympic sprint to get out of her mouth.

'Slow down,' I said. 'What's going on?'

'I asked her,' Aura said. 'About Amma living in your grandparents' house. A part of me still couldn't completely believe it, you see. But I told her the address. And it's true. But then out of nowhere I felt like a dragon had set a fire in my belly. I just got mad. I mean, how could she have sold the house, knowing the dragons were growing and Amma wasn't there to look after them? She was acting like she didn't even know what was in her own garden.'

'Maybe she didn't,' I said.

'How could she not? Amma knew. She showed me the dragons. Why wouldn't she have shown her own daughter?'

I shrugged.

'I couldn't believe she'd kept that from me, or that she'd walked away from the dragons. At first I was tiptoeing around, asking what if we'd left something behind, something important. But she insisted that it was just a house and a garden. So then . . .' She paused. 'Then I did something you're not going to like.'

I looked at her and she bit the corner of her lip.

'I asked her straight out about the dragons. About Amma growing dragons and looking after them.'

'Aura!' I cried. 'How could you?!'

'I know. I'm sorry. The thing is, she just smiled. And started acting as if they were just Amma's stories.'

For a second I relaxed. Until Aura spoke again.

'So I did something you're really not going to like.'

'What?'

'I did a blurt,' she said. 'Like you did when you showed me Zing.'

I took a step back, remembering how I'd got cross and stormed into my room with a bemused Aura trailing behind and flung the toy box open. To prove a point.

'What did you do?' I stared at her waiting for the words to drop like concrete bricks on my feet.

'I showed her Rosebud,' Aura said. She was biting her whole lip now and her face had escalated to way beyond even a grimace.

'You what?' I spluttered.

'Hold on,' Aura pleaded. 'That's not the thing.'

'That's quite a Thing,' I blustered. 'Giving up the secret of the dragons. That's a giant-sized Thing with a capital "TH". What were you thinking?'

'She didn't see Rosebud,' Aura said quietly.

'Good. Well, at least that's something,' I said, still cross.

'No, I mean she didn't *see* her. Rosebud was right there on my hand and Mamma was looking directly at her. She even fluttered all around her head! But Mamma didn't – I don't know, couldn't – see her.'

'I don't understand,' I said.

'No,' Aura agreed. 'Nor do I. It was like Rosebud just didn't exist for her.'

11
Zing Leads the Way

During school, at every possible opportunity, Aura unleashed question after question about Elvi and Arturo. She'd spent the whole evening poring over her grandmother's diaries. I have to admit it had been a bit of a wrench, handing over the box of Elvi's things before we left Nana and Grandad's the previous day. But they clearly belonged to Aura now, so what could I do?

'We have to find out if there are any more things hidden away,' she said over the lunch table in an urgent hushed voice. 'I want to know why Mamma can't see the dragons. Maybe something happened to her? And maybe Amma knew. She might have written about it. There just has to be another hiding place in the house or garden. Perhaps I'll remember something if we go back again. It's worth a try.'

When the bell finally rang, we all rushed straight to Nana and Grandad's. I didn't need convincing to go hunting again. I wasn't sure Rosebud's breath had helped the seedling. In fact, one of the leaves was already going brown around the edges. The sooner we found Arturo's letters the better. Assuming, of course, that there were letters to be found.

'What are you doing?' Aura said, as we stood together in the garden. Liam was dangling a magnet in the shape of a cat on a piece of string in front of her face.

'Hypnotising you,' he declared. 'To unlock your memories. I've seen someone do it on the telly.'

Aura rolled her eyes and pushed his hand away.

'We found the other things under the floor of the shed,' I added, 'but I've looked and looked and there's nothing else there. Can you remember anything? Maybe you saw her hiding stuff?'

Aura didn't reply. She was scanning the garden. We waited, watching the concentration on her face finally flicker to frustration.

'Nothing,' she said sadly. 'I don't remember ever seeing her hide anything. Not in the house and not here. I thought it might come flooding back like before, but I just don't think there is anything to remember.' She slumped down on the bench. 'I'm sorry, Tomas.'

Suddenly Zing zoomed down from a branch and darted past her head, clipping her with one of his wings.

'Ow,' she said. 'He buzzed me.'

I watched Zing as he started dive-bombing the compost heap. Something he'd been doing rather a lot lately, now I came to think of it. He paused, then darted back, and this time he gave me a quick sharp shock, before he zoomed off again. We watched him hopping up and down on the pile of compost, eyes fixed on us. What was he playing at? What was so important about a heap of compost?

Then my eyes fell on the shed. And suddenly I got it!

'Hang on!' I cried suddenly. 'When we were here yesterday, you said there were two sheds. Not one.'

Ted, Liam and Aura exchanged a look, eyes wide.

With a jolt I remembered Grandad once saying they'd pulled down another shed when they first moved in, because one of the back panels had been damaged.

We all raced over to Zing.

'The floor of the shed would have been right underneath the compost heap,' I said, excitement spilling out like froth from a shaken can. 'I bet that's where the hidey hole is!'

'Do you think Zing knew all along?' Aura said, pointing at the dragon, who was hopping up and down and jabbing at the heap with his tail.

'It's possible,' Ted said. 'Sharks have a sixth sense;

they can detect electric charge. Maybe Zing's like that and could sense what's buried.'

'He was with me that day I looked under Grandad's shed,' I said. 'And he was acting weird then, flying at the compost. I thought it was just, you know, Zing being Zing.'

I looked over at him and gave him an apologetic shrug. He flared bright silver and disappeared, only to reappear above my head. His tail batted my arm and a little zap of electricity buzzed me. I laughed. 'Next time I'll listen, I promise.'

'Right, who's going in?' Liam asked. 'That stuff reeks.'

'That's because it's got manure in there too,' I said.

'Oh, great,' Ted said. 'More poo.'

Aura and I grabbed a spade each and started digging, heaping the compost into Grandad's barrow for Ted and

Liam to wheel away, while Zing darted to and fro above us. By the time we'd cleared the side nearest the shed, uncovering old wooden floorboards, we were all sweating and groaning and Ted was mumbling about the lack of cake. I had to admit I could have done with some water and maybe one of Grandad's caramel toffees.

'I hope you're right about this,' Liam said.

I looked at Zing, who had just flown down and was hopping towards the back of the heap. He paused and then started scratching frantically at the compost.

'I think we're close,' I said. 'OK, Zing,' I whispered. 'I'm listening. Let me get in there with my spade.'

Zing turned, fluttered up and clung to my back. His eyes fixed on the point where my spade had just dug in.

I pulled it out and Aura and I looked at each other as we heard a scrape of metal on metal.

'There was a handle on the loose floorboard in Grandad's shed,' I gasped.

Aura thrust her spade in and together we cleared

the space, revealing the wood underneath. And there, sticking out of one plank, was a metal ring.

12
Treasure!

'What is it?' Liam asked, craning over my shoulder. 'What's in there?'

Having pulled up the wooden board, we were all peering down into a hole. It was bigger than the hole under Grandad's shed, but this one looked empty. I sank back onto my heels and let out a groan of frustration.

But then Zing hopped inside the hole, lighting it up as the silver threads in his wings and body flared brightly.

'Look, there,' Aura said, and she began to scrape away at one side of the hole. Dirt cascaded down over her hands until suddenly we saw the edge of what looked like a wooden box. 'Help me pull it out,' she cried.

I leaned in and together we dragged the box up and out.

I remembered how exciting it had felt to find the 'treasure' buried under Grandad's shed. As I looked around at Liam, Ted and Aura, I knew this time I wasn't the only one jiggling.

No one spoke as we lifted the lid. I reached in and pulled out a stack of letters. Flicking through them I felt a grin bound onto my face like an over-excited puppy.

'They're from Arturo!' I squeaked.

'And there's another diary!' Aura said, waving a notebook in the air, delighted.

'What on earth is that?' Liam asked pointing at a slightly shrivelled pod-like thing, about the size of my head. 'Is it a dried-up dragon fruit?'

I took the pod from him and examined it. 'I suppose it could be. But it doesn't look quite the right shape.'

Ted was shaking a tin to his ear. 'Hey, there's something rattling in here.' He tried to peel the lid off, but let out his breath in a gasp as he failed to undo it.

He passed the tin to me, and I levered the lid off with the edge of a trowel. Inside were beans. They looked a bit like the coffee beans Mum grinds up to make what she calls 'proper coffee'.

'Look at this,' Aura said quietly. 'It's a picture of my abuelo.' She held out a photograph that had slipped from between the pages of the diary. 'He's my grandfather,' she added, showing the picture to Liam and Ted.

I took the photo from her and stared down at it. A man with short black hair and a wide smile was standing outside a house, one hand on a fence and the other resting on the shoulder of another man with a close-cropped beard. A man I recognised.

'That's Arturo,' I said.

'So they did know each other,' Ted said.

'I guess so.'

I opened my rucksack and slid Arturo's letters inside. Then I looked up and saw Aura watching me.

'Just for tonight, so I can read them,' I explained, suddenly wondering if I actually had the right to take them away.

'OK, great. I'll have plenty to read with this,' Aura replied. She'd already turned back to the diary and was flicking through it. She paused, then held it up, a finger pointing to a drawing on one of the pages.

'I don't believe it – it's the dragon,' she said. 'The one I always draw. The one with four wings.'

I stared at the pencil sketch in the diary. She was right. It looked exactly like the dragon I'd seen in the pictures stuck up all over Aura's bedroom walls.

I swallowed the rather large lump in my throat and felt it sink down into the hollow pit of my stomach.

It was clearer than ever that Aura's history with the dragons went back long before I ever came into the garden.

13
Doubts and Dumplings

That night I had a dream. I was in Grandad's garden. I could see the fruit trees reaching their crooked arms out towards me, and feel the brambly fingers of the hedge scratching at my coat as I stood on the fringe of the veggie plot.

Aura was over by the dragon-fruit tree. Dragons flew all around her, flitting past her head and landing on her outstretched hands.

She was laughing in delight.

I opened my mouth to call to her and tried to go to join her by the tree, but my voice sounded tiny, like a weeny ant with a sore throat. And my feet were heavy with mud, rooting me to the spot.

All I could do was watch as dragon after dragon flew to her, their sparks dancing in the air, leaving me forgotten on the sidelines, slowly disappearing under a tangle of weeds.

OK, so sometimes dreams can be weird and difficult to fathom, but other times they're crystal clear. Waking up, I knew that Liam's words had sown a seed in my head, a seed that had quickly grown into that tangle of weeds. Was he right? Would Aura take her rightful crown as Queen of the Dragons? After all, she was Elvi's granddaughter. And they had grown dragons long before we had. It was her tree. Her dragons.

Before my head took me places I didn't want to go, I needed to talk to someone about all this. And I knew just who that someone was. Two someones in fact. I looked at my watch: 5.50 a.m. Good. Kat and Kai should be on their lunch break. With the time difference, we'd had to work out when we could talk on the computer. And luckily first thing in the morning was one of those times.

I sent a request and waited, tapping the table.

Zing flew down and clung to my back, his head resting against my neck and his tail thumping me gently. His wings were spread out so I could see the tips of them sprouting from my shoulders. As the twins appeared on screen, I waved, letting out a sigh of relief.

'Hello from Suzhou,' Kat said.

'All right?' I replied. 'What's up with Kai?' I said watching him wince his way through a mouthful of his lunch. 'Don't you like the food there or something?'

'The opposite.' Kat laughed. 'He burned his mouth on a shengjian bao at breakfast this morning. Couldn't cram it in fast enough.'

Kai mumbled something.

'Yeah, I like dumplings too, but that's not why Tomas is calling us. Look at him, it's like he's been sat on by that Tyrannodragon and then had a poo explode all over him. What's happened, Tomas?'

I told them all about Aura and Elvi and how we'd unearthed the rest of the things Elvi had hidden.

'So Aura's really Elvi's granddaughter? That's amazing,' Kat exclaimed, and Kai nodded.

'Yeah,' I agreed. 'Really amazing.'

Kat's face loomed large as she peered into the screen. It took me by surprise and I leaned away, almost falling backwards off my chair.

'You're worried, aren't you?' she said.

There was no point hiding it. I nodded.

'What about?'

It was a good question. What exactly was making my stomach so squirmy? It was probably time I had a good look, rather than just shoving the uncomfortable feelings I'd been living with under the rug and

pretending they weren't there at all.

'I found the tree in Grandad's garden,' I said slowly. 'And now . . . Well, what if Aura wants to take it away? I mean, it was Elvi's garden after all. And she was her grandma. Really the tree belongs to Aura.'

'Come on, Tomas. It doesn't belong to anyone,' Kat said. 'I get it, I really do, but from what you've said, I don't think Aura sees it like that at all. You can trust her. Just like Elvi trusted Arturo.'

'Course you can,' Kai insisted. 'Now shut up and listen to this. We've found dragons!'

As my eyes widened, Kat elbowed him and laughed.

'What do you mean?' I said. 'For real?'

'Well, maybe,' Kai said sheepishly. 'Once upon a time.'

It turned out that when Crystal and Dodger had found their way to the twins, they had flown them over Shanghai, landing in the Yuyuan Garden.

'The garden is so beautiful,' Kat said. 'There are all these bridges and colourful pagodas and –'

'And dragon walls,' butted in Kai.

Kat looked at him crossly. 'Can I ever just finish my own sentence?'

'We've seen plenty of dragon fruits too,' Kai went on. 'They sell them at the market. And we saw a tree poking over the wall of someone's garden.'

I raised my eyebrows.

'I don't think any of them are active,' Kat said quickly.

'Not that we know about,' Kai piped up. 'But who knows what we'll find? I'm leaving no dragon-fruit tree unchecked for as long as we're here!'

14
Is That a Dragon on Your Head?

Although I'm used to seeing my mum with a cockatoo on her head, I still wasn't prepared to see Aura's mum with a dragon on hers.

When I called round at their house on Sunday, Rosa opened the door wearing a brightly patterned dress and a yellow beret with Rosebud sitting comfortably on top of the hat. My eyes flicked to Aura, who was half tumbling down the stairs towards us, fizzy with excitement.

'Don't you like it?' Rosa asked, touching the sides of her beret.

'Er . . . yes,' I said, realising I'd been staring at her head.

Rosa closed the door and turned to admire her hat in the hall mirror.

'Are you sure she can't see Rosebud?' I whispered to Aura, who was grinning widely.

'Positive,' she said. 'Watch this.'

She lifted a hand and Rosebud launched herself off Rosa's head and flew to and fro right in front of her. The little dragon even did a somersault, but Rosa didn't bat an eyelid.

'Hey, Mamma, what was that? Something just flew past your head,' Aura said with a giggle.

'What?' Rosa spun around. 'Was it a bird? We had one in here the other day. Must have flown in and got stuck.'

'There it is!' Aura said.

Rosa looked hard at the spot where Rosebud was hovering.

'I can't see anything. Maybe it already flew out.'

'Nope, it's right there on the end of your nose. I think it might actually be a dragon, not a bird.'

Rosa laughed. 'You and your dragon stories. Next you'll be telling me Tomas has one in his pocket.'

'You do, don't you, Tomas?' Aura said. 'Go on – why don't you introduce Zing.'

Aura pulled at my pocket where Zing was tucked safely away. And before I could stop her, Zing had peeked his head out, seen Rosebud careering around above us and zoomed up to join her.

I glanced at Rosa. But she was still smiling fondly at Aura.

As Zing darted up and down the stairs, he knocked a picture with his tail. It fell with a crash to the floor.

'Bother,' Rosa said. 'I've been meaning to fix that frame for weeks.'

Aura looked at me and shrugged. 'Always finds something to explain it away,' she said.

'I'll clear it up after we've eaten. Hope you're both hungry,' Rosa said.

Aura grabbed my sleeve as I began to make my way through to the kitchen. 'Listen,' she hissed. 'Eat quickly, OK? I've got something to tell you once we're on our own. And Mamma might not be able to see stuff, but she can still hear.'

Having tea with Rosa while the two little dragons whizzed around the kitchen felt strange. At one point Rosebud perched on the fruit bowl, flicking her tail back and forth across Rosa's plate. We watched, trying not to laugh as every time she took a mouthful the tail just missed her fork. Until finally a mistimed swipe hit it and sent her food flying across the table.

'I'm ever so clumsy at the moment,' Rosa said. 'Yesterday I knocked a whole pot of yogurt across the room!' We sniggered as Rosa apologised yet again for her sudden strange food flinging when another forkful splatted against the fridge.

It actually felt amazing not having to hide the dragons, and a relief not to always be on my guard. We could just sit back and enjoy watching them zooming around us, and when they settled on our arm or shoulder I didn't have to keep one eye standing firmly to attention. But every so often I couldn't help noticing Aura's smile slip, and I wondered if actually she'd prefer it if her mum could share in the joke.

It turned out I was right. As soon as we were up in her room she asked, 'Don't you ever wish you could share the dragons with your mum and dad? I can't help wishing Mamma could see Rosebud. And Papi too. I bet he wouldn't have any trouble seeing her.'

I looked at her, alarmed. Was she planning on telling her dad?

'You know you can't tell him? We have to protect the dragons – we can't go telling more people about them.'

'I know,' she said quickly. 'It's just that you're lucky you've got your grandad. And Lolli,' she added.

She did have a point. 'I know. I'm sorry. Don't forget you have the superhero squad though.'

Aura smiled and gave a nod.

'Hey, you said you had something you needed to tell me.'

'Yeah, I do.' She leaped up, starting to get fizzy again, and reached under the pillow on her bed.

'I was reading Amma's diary last night. And I found out that Mamma definitely used to be able to see the dragons. You know that picture I always draw? Well, it turns out it's her dragon. She actually had a dragon! But then one day she couldn't see it any more; she couldn't see any dragons. Or even remember that they existed in real life. Amma was really sad. She couldn't work out what had happened. After that she and Mamma were never quite as close, because Amma couldn't share the dragons she loved so much with her. Maybe that's why she always told me about the dragon, to keep it alive for Mamma in case one day she remembered.'

Aura gave a little shrug. 'It makes me feel a bit sad too.' She looked up and sighed. 'But don't worry, I won't tell Papi.'

Before I could say anything else, Rosa popped her head in. 'Anyone fancy watching a film?'

'Thanks,' I said, 'but I'd better go, I promised Lolli we'd finish building her Lego space station. She's supposed to be taking it into school tomorrow and her arm still hurts, so she needs a bit of help.'

'Oh dear – what happened to her arm?' Rosa asked.

'I think it's from when she went for a burton in the garden.'

'A what-on?' Aura said.

I smiled. 'Just something Grandad says. She went flying. Don't you remember?'

Aura nodded. 'Poor Lolli. I hope she hasn't fractured it – I did that once and it hurt like mad.'

I frowned. 'I'd have thought Mum and Dad would have got it checked out if it was that bad.'

'Well, give her this from me,' Aura said. And she handed me a picture she'd drawn of Rosebud. 'Actually, hang on.' She grabbed it back and for the next couple of minutes she huddled over the paper, pen in hand.

When she held it up I saw she'd drawn herself next to Rosebud, and Lolli and Tinkle too. And she'd written: 'To Lolli, I hope your arm feels better soon. Love Aura.'

'She'll love it,' I said, smiling. 'Thanks.'

15
Ouchy

On the way home from Aura's house I saw a familiar figure getting off the Number 6 bus. I don't know about you, but I always find it a bit weird seeing someone out of the place you usually see them. It's like when you meet a teacher outside of school. Somehow I have this idea that they just live there, in special teacher containment pods. So seeing Chouko was a bit like that, because up till then I'd only ever seen her in the botanic garden, surrounded by trees and plants. Standing there, she looked like a flower that had been uprooted and left on the pavement.

'Chouko!' I called, and hurried towards her.

'Ah, hello, Tomas,' she said.

I couldn't help noticing she looked tired.

'Would you like a hand?' I said, eyeing the huge bag she was carrying.

'Oh, I'm fine, thank you,' she replied. 'Just a long and rather exhausting day. One of those where everyone and everything seems to need you at once. And some people like to think they know what's best. Even though it's your work they're meddling with,' she added.

I nodded, not really listening. I was too eager to ask the question jumping up and down in my head.

'How are the seedlings doing?'

She gave a little sigh. 'Not so well, actually. They were one of the things that were being rather demanding.'

'What do you mean?' I asked quickly. 'I thought they looked healthy last time I saw them?'

'Yes, they were. But they've all gone a bit limp. Rather like me,' she said with a little laugh.

'But what are we going to do?' I squeaked. I realised by the look on Chouko's face that the words had come out sounding as desperate as I now felt.

'I'm sure I'll figure it out,' she said. 'Although some plants just don't thrive, whatever you do. I don't like to admit defeat, but sometimes there's not a lot to be done.'

'You mustn't give up on them,' I pleaded. She took a little step back as if I might grab hold of her in my desperation.

'I'll certainly do my best, Tomas. Better get off now though. Your parents must be expecting you.'

Back at home, I hurried upstairs. I passed Lolli's room, but I was so preoccupied, imagining the seedlings shrivelling up and dying, that I didn't see Lolli at first. Then again, I'm not sure I would have spotted her even if I had been taking notice. She'd made a huge nest on her bedroom floor with a quilt, several blankets and what looked like every pillow in the house. She was half buried under a pile of cuddlies and a huge bunch of sticks, most of which had plasters stuck all over them. A piece of paper was taped to the floor, and on it she'd drawn a big red cross in crayon and lines of little sticks with smiley faces. To be honest, her sticky hospital was looking a bit overcrowded. Then a little white tail bobbed up and I realised Mr Floppybobbington was in there too.

'You OK, Lollibob?' I asked. 'Thought you wanted some help with your space station?'

Lolli looked up and gave a long sigh. 'We're all too hurty for making fings,' she said.

Dad popped his head out of the bathroom and, seeing me, came over carrying a huge basket of washing.

'Poor Lolli – she's not feeling too well. Wouldn't even eat my special spaghetti.'

'Why has she got all the sticks in with her like that?' I said quietly.

'Oh, Mum was telling her about imprinting. You know, when baby animals attach to the parents when

they're born. There was this one girl who hatched a gaggle of goslings and they all thought she was their mum. So Lolli's now convinced Mr Floppybobbington and all the poorly sticks have imprinted on her. She won't go anywhere without them.'

Lolli gave a little grunt and held up her arm with the other hand to show me.

'Is it still sore?' I asked.

She nodded and stuck out her little bottom lip. 'It's all ouchy. Can you do us singing, Tomas?' she asked. 'Herbert needs a lullyby, but all my singsong has gone.'

'I'm not sure my singing is very comforting,' I teased. 'I might scare him.'

'But you do good songs,' she insisted. 'And it will help, promise.'

'Come on, she needs an early night, Tomas,' Dad said.

'Another time,' I replied. 'You need to sleep now.'

Lolli yawned and pointed to one of the sticks, which had fallen from the cosy nest. 'Need Douglas,' she said quietly. I reached down and picked it – him – up. Poor Douglas was more plaster than stick, as far as I could tell.

I tucked him in beside her.

'Night night, Lollibob,' I said. And then remembering Aura's picture, I laid it next to her, and immediately regretted it as her eyes started to shine with tears.

'Tinkle,' she whispered.

'You'll see her soon,' I promised.

16
Letters from Arturo

Later, after Mum and Dad had said goodnight, I switched on my rocket lamp, pulled out my rucksack and spread the letters we'd found across the quilt. Zing, who'd been curled up in one of my jumpers, launched himself upwards and landed on my back. He wriggled, getting comfy, and I winced a bit, feeling his claws through my pyjamas.

'Right, time to get reading,' I whispered. Zing rubbed the bottom of his jaw across my shoulder and bashed me a couple of times with his tail. The air crackled and I felt some of my hair stand on end.

I just hoped our excitement was warranted and Arturo
could tell us what we needed to know.

I started to read, and the hours slipped by. It was clear
that Arturo loved the forest and all that it contained. And
his letters were crammed with scribbled notes telling Elvi
about what he'd seen and learned. But the pages were
full of his worries too, about keeping the Hidden Dragon

City secret from developers, who were moving deeper and deeper into the forest. There was too much at stake he said, too much that could be lost forever.

Sometimes I turned a page and saw that he'd decorated the margins with drawings. On one, he'd sketched a tree with strange pods, draping over the page, its branches intertwining with the words so that it looked as if his writing and his thoughts grew from this tree.

My eyes lit up when he said:

I have found more writing carved into stones in this temple. I believe now that the two seeds we found resting in the golden dragon foot were not the last two active dragon-fruit seeds. I believe there was a third placed there. It may simply have fallen right here, knocked from its resting place by an inquisitive animal. I am searching every day, inch by inch, hoping against hope I will find it. Because this time I know what I need to do to help it grow.

But if I find nothing I will search into the forest beyond. For maybe someone has already taken it and it is growing safe and strong somewhere out there.

Either way, I will not stop searching. One day, my dear friend, I hope I too will grow dragons

I felt a buzz, and this time it wasn't Zing! I was right, he did know something!

But as I read on, there was more and more about the customs and history of the people from the Hidden City and how they looked after all sorts of other trees and plants, and nothing at all about what he would do differently if he ever found the seed. I dropped the letters in frustration, my eyes burning from reading so late. I wriggled down under the covers to try to get some sleep, but instead lay there tossing and turning for hours.

When I crawled out of bed the next morning I found
the house quiet. Lolli was still curled up in her nest,
not belting around the kitchen with her cape flying out
behind her as usual.

Mum was on the phone and Dad was getting
breakfast ready.

'Lolli still not feeling well?' I asked.

He shook his head sadly. 'I even made Douglas and
Herbert some breakfast,' he said, pointing at two little
bottle caps filled with dollops of gloopy porridge. 'But
she still wouldn't get up. We're going to take her to A &
E, in case she needs an X-ray on her arm or anything.'

When I went up to see her after my cereal, I
discovered Lolli wasn't too sure about her 'eggy ray'. So
I said she could take Pink Dog – who has lived in my
bed since I was four and doesn't go anywhere usually
because she's totally not brave enough to go out. (Some
people can be really mean when you're pink.) Luckily

for Pink Dog, Lolli just said, ''S'OK, Tomas, I got all the sticks coming.'

Before setting off for school, I tucked Arturo's letters into my rucksack. Halfway down the street, I met Ted.

'I wish I hadn't fallen asleep,' I said, after telling him about my late night of reading.

'So Arturo didn't say what he'd learned then?'

I shook my head. 'I guess it might still be in there, hidden among the scribbles and drawings and stuff. I'll just have to keep looking.'

Just like Arturo, I thought to myself.

'He spent more time talking about cacao trees – whatever they are – than dragon-fruit trees,' I added.

Ted looked dreamy. 'Mmmm,' he said. 'Chocolate.'

I looked at him a bit crossly, 'Can you not focus on anything other than chocolate? This is important.'

'I am! The cacao tree is another name for the cocoa tree – you know, that thing that gives us the beans chocolate's made with,' he said, rolling his eyes. 'Besides why shouldn't I focus on chocolate? Chocolate fixes everything.'

I laughed. If only.

17
A Cloud of Dragons

Towards the end of the day a note came from the office for me. Miss Jelinski called me to her desk to say that Mum had phoned and they were still at the hospital with Lolli, so I should go straight to Nana and Grandad's after school.

I was glad the rest of the superhero squad were free to come with me. I suddenly felt a bit wobbly at the thought of Lolli in hospital. Even with her sticks to keep her company, I knew she wouldn't like it.

'I'm not sure what the doctors will make of all her sticky patients,' I said, and quickly explained how

Dad had told her about imprinting and how she was so attached we couldn't get her to leave them behind.

'The doctor won't mind a few sticks. They'll probably all come back covered in stickers,' Liam said.

'I'm sure she'll be OK,' Aura said, giving me a reassuring smile.

I nodded, hoping she was right. Poorly seedlings were bad enough, without a poorly Lolli as well.

'I think I imprinted on a doughnut this morning,' Ted added, giving me a grin. 'I definitely found it hard to leave it behind.'

When we got to Grandad's garden, it was raining steadily. We squelched our way over to the dragon-fruit tree.

'It's a bit soggy round here,' I said.

'We've been having a lot of dawn downpours,' Grandad said. 'But it's all been clear skies by the time you pop your head out of bed, so I don't expect you've noticed.'

'Do you think the tree will be OK?' I asked remembering Chouko's warning about cacti not liking to get their feet wet.

'No, I don't think it will,' he said. 'But don't you worry, Chipstick. I've got a plan. And now you're all here, we can get to work on it.'

He handed Liam and Ted a garden fork each.

'Right, you two, you're on spike duty. We need lots of little holes all across the grass. That'll stop the ground from getting too waterlogged. Tomas, you and me are going to dig out a little pond over at the back there. That's a good spot for wildlife and it'll give the water somewhere to drain to.'

'What about me?' Aura asked.

'Compost,' Grandad said. 'Grab that wheelbarrow and start spreading it all over. And you can take a closer look at the tree while you're doing it. Give us a yell if you see any yellowing leaves.'

When Aura gave a yelp soon after, I was afraid she'd found something wrong with the tree. I dropped my spade and sploshed over to her.

'What is it? What's wrong with it?'

'Nothing,' she said. 'Sorry. I just got a bit of a surprise.'

She pulled back one of the cactus leaves and out flew about a dozen teeny tiny dragons. They were only as big as my thumb. And they had long pointed snouts and were all different colours, although they shared the same glittery orange wings. They hovered in front of Aura's face in a little cluster.

'Wow, they're beautiful,' I said. They were like little shiny jewels.

'And so tiny,' Aura agreed, smiling. 'And there's more too.'

I peered back in past the cactus leaves and saw other tiny dragons darting in and out.

'I spotted this one fruit that was a bit bigger than all the rest,' she said. 'And it was yellower than the really red ripe ones. I thought maybe it'd been damaged, especially after what your grandad said about looking for yellow leaves. It was lying on the wet ground too, so I moved it so it could rest on one of these flowerpots. Only it burst.' She grinned as several of the dragons fluttered down and settled on her hair. 'And it was packed full of these little beauties.'

'There must be at least fifty,' I said.

The flurry of little dragons joined together in a shimmering cloud of colour. We watched as they settled on the flowerpot and then laughed as it started lifting off the ground as they rose into the air. It swung there precariously until Liam and Ted appeared behind us to see what was going on and startled the dragons so that they shot off in all directions, sending the pot tumbling back down with a splash.

I noticed several of the dragons taking a keen interest in the winter pansies, their long yellow tongues shooting out of their mouths as they hovered over them.

'They're like hummingbirds,' Liam said.

'Yeah, but they're even smaller than bee hummingbirds,' Ted said.

'I didn't even know that was a thing,' I replied.

'Sure is,' Ted said, taking a breath as he revved up for a full-on fact frenzy. 'Bee hummingbirds are the smallest bird in the world. They're about six centimetres long, a bit rounder and plumper than these but they're just as colourful. Found across the entire Cuban archipelago. Often mistaken for insects.' He took another breath and then said with total glee, 'Their heart rate can reach 1,260 beats per minute. And they can flap their wings at eighty beats per second! And this is the best bit – they can fly upside down and backwards!'

We all turned and stared at the flitting dragons.

'It looks like these guys can too,' Liam cried, delighted.

Sure enough a few of the dragons had started doing some pretty spectacular aerial acrobatics.

'They're like a display team, I said, laughing.

When we went back to our tasks, the dragons flitted back and forth over Aura's head. They followed

her as she wheeled in another barrow of compost,
little flecks of colour glimmering in the light of the late
afternoon.

'Better get that pond dug,' Grandad said, looking up
at the sky. 'Reckon we'll be getting another downpour
tonight.'

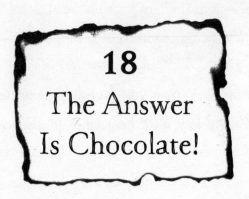

18
The Answer
Is Chocolate!

Squashed in Grandad's shed later, we sheltered from the rain. The wooden box we'd found buried under the compost heap sat on the table in front of us. We had each found something to read and no one was saying much, mainly because our mouths were too full of Nana's jam tarts.

I'd found another one of Arturo's letters tucked into an envelope of photos. As my eyes flicked down the paper in my hand, I suddenly spluttered crumbs.

'Listen to this,' I said. 'Arturo's talking about Rosa not being able to see the dragons.'

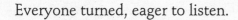

Everyone turned, eager to listen.

Dear Elvi, I have been thinking of what you told me, how you found Rosa staring up at the sky that day, how when you lifted her mask she looked as if she was in a trance. I just wish I could help you both. But I don't understand why she would stop being able to see the dragons. I know how hard it must be for you, my dear friend, when only hours before she was tearing around the garden, leaping out at the dragons in her costume, having such fun. And then to have her simply laugh when you asked her about her dragon, as if you were making a joke, as if it was just a part of the Halloween party games

I turned the page over, but it was blank. I riffled through the photos but there was no sign of another page of the letter.

Aura's shoulders sagged. 'I really hoped he'd be able to tell us what had happened.'

The door squeaked open and Grandad squeezed in carrying a tray full of pots. He put it on the counter, disturbing a layer of dust along with the uncomfortable silence that had settled over us.

'Is it me or is this shed shrinking?' he said. 'I'm sure there used to be more room in here – even with you lot in it.'

'I think we've just grown a bit,' Ted said with a grin.

'*You* have anyway,' I said. Ted was about a foot taller than me and seemed to show no signs of slowing down. 'I'm still waiting for my growth spurt,' I added.

Grandad winked at me. 'It'll come, Chipstick,' he said. 'Some things just take their time.'

He glanced down at the box. 'What've you got there then?'

I explained about the letter and the other new treasure we'd found.

Liam waved the shrivelled pod in the air. 'Course, it's not exactly buried gold.' He laughed.

'Next best thing, by the looks of it,' Grandad chuckled. 'Bet Lolli would think chocolate was treasure anyway.'

I looked at him, confused.

'That *is* a cocoa pod, isn't it?' Grandad said.

And suddenly, like the counters in a game of Connect 4 dropping into place, an image of the letters from Arturo that I'd been reading last night flashed into my jam-tart-powered mind. I'd been carrying them around all day and now I grabbed them from my bag.

While everyone looked on in confusion, I flicked through until I found the one I'd been looking for. The one where Arturo had drawn a tree interweaving his words. I held it out to everyone.

'Look – it's got pods on it, just like this. It must be the cacao tree he was talking about. Arturo DID tell me the answer!' I cried.

I rummaged in the box until I found the tin with the beans in, levered off the lid and thrust it under Grandad's nose.

'We thought these were coffee beans,' I said excitedly. 'But I don't think they are. I think they're cocoa beans, from the cocoa pod.'

Everyone was still looking at me like I had lost the plot. So I slowed down. 'I was telling Ted that in his letters Arturo wrote loads about cacao trees. He went on about how they grew alongside the dragon-fruit trees and they were really important to the people in the Hidden

City. They had customs and rituals based around them and everything. But I totally missed why Arturo was so interested. What if he'd figured out that the thing dragon-fruit seedlings need to grow well is the *cacao*?'

'You mean they like chocolate too?' Liam said.

'Well, if it's good enough for Grandad's garden,' I said happily, remembering the cocoa mulch he'd been spreading.

'That's why it was important to the people of the Hidden City, and why Arturo was talking about it in the letters, and why Elvi had a tin of cocoa beans hidden away!'

'Hang on,' Aura suddenly said, examining Arturo's drawing. 'That tree looks like the one in the botanic garden, the one the seedlings were growing on.'

I grabbed the letter and stared at it.

'You're right!' I cried. 'That's why the seedlings were doing so well in there.'

Ted grinned. 'I *told* you the answer is always chocolate!'

19
A Sad Sing-Song

'Nothing broken,' Mum said as I clambered into the car later.

She smiled and looked over at Lolli, who was clutching sticky Herbert and staring out the window at the sky.

'That's great news,' I said. 'Isn't it, Lolli?'

Lolli turned and gave me a little nodling. I wasn't used to her being so quiet. Usually as soon as I stepped into the car she'd have been rattling off a huge list of everything that had happened at the hospital.

She pulled back the blanket she'd laid over the sticky patients resting on the back seat between us and then looked at me expectantly. 'So they can hear the singing that you sing,' she said.

It looked as if I was going to have to keep my promise and sing her a get-well song. I half hummed, half sang a few lines of 'Puff the Magic Dragon' – it wasn't exactly in Tinkle's league, but it seemed to cheer her up a bit. And that made me feel better too.

When we got home I left Mum and Dad to put Lolli to bed and headed to my room, where the little seedling was still sitting sadly in the pot of earth. Although I wasn't exactly sure how the dragon-fruit and the cacao trees worked together, I figured I'd try crumbling the beans into the soil. I told the little plant the story of our chocolate discovery – if Chouko was right and stories really did help, then surely it'd love this one! I couldn't help feeling excited – if I could figure out how to look after the seedlings, I really would have earned back the title of Grand High DragonMaster!

'So, what *is* the problem, if it's not broken?' I asked Mum later when she and Dad came to say goodnight.

'I expect she just bruised it,' Mum said. 'And it'll be sore for a bit.'

'But when she fell off that trampoline at Bea's party and smashed her front tooth, there was blood everywhere. It must have been really sore for days with her lip cut like that; she cried for a bit when it happened, but then she didn't seem to care.' I paused. 'So her arm must be pretty bad.'

Mum leaned down and hugged me.

'Let's hope she feels better in the morning once she's had a good sleep.'

'How about I ask everyone to meet here

tomorrow? Maybe she'll perk up, with the superhero squad looking after her.'

'Maybe,' Mum said. 'But let's see how she is. She might just need a quiet day.'

Dad bent down and did his best rock 'n' roll tuck-in.

'How did you get to be such a good big brother, hey, Tomas?'

'By having such a good little sister,' I whispered.

I lay in bed and watched Zing fly to and fro. But I couldn't sleep. I wriggled out and crept into Lolli's room. She was tucked up in a Dad-made cocoon, but she was wide awake and she'd obviously been crying. She screwed up her face and started judder-crying when she saw me. I had a feeling this was going get loud.

I quickly started whisper-singing,

calm her down. It did, thank goodness, but she didn't look very sleepy.

'Want to hear a story all about chocolate?' I said.

She nodded and I grabbed one of the quilts from her nest and scooched in beside her, careful not to bump her sore arm.

I think I'd reached the part where Arturo found the cacao trees when Lolli fell asleep.

That night I had a dream.

I was somewhere dark – and a bit smelly too. It smelled like the time Tomtom had batted a rotten egg and it had smashed and got all over his fur. I reached out my hand and touched rock.

I don't usually mind the dark, but this was different. It was so hot it was stifling, and when I tried to talk my words sounded all short and muffled like there was nowhere for them to go. I felt squashed.

I didn't like this dark.

And then I heard a rumble and a long sonorous note that had all kinds of sad running through it.

I stepped forward, but I banged my head and had to stoop, lower and lower until finally I was crawling on my belly with the sharp rock crushing me on all sides. I could feel something flapping wildly inside me, like a trapped bird. I wanted to open my mouth and let it out, but my lips were clamped shut. I started to hum, hoping it would calm me like it had calmed Lolli. The hum echoed around me.

And suddenly Zing was there with me. He flared brightly, and I could see my way. I felt his little buzz and knew I wasn't on my own. The flapping bird inside me settled. Slowly, inch by inch, I wriggled forward, until the rock above stopped clawing at my hair and I could lift my head, then finally crawl on my hands and knees.

I could still hear the long sad note. It rang off the walls now as if it was searching for me. It was getting clearer. And clearer. And I hummed louder in response, until the two notes met and joined. All at once the tunnel widened and I saw daylight high above me. And there curled on the ground, caught in the beams of light, was the silvery blue shape of a dragon.

Slowly the dragon lifted its head and stared sadly up towards the sky.

20
Dreaming with Dragons

'I had this awful dream last night,' I told everyone the next afternoon.

'I used to have a really bad dream,' Liam said, jumping in. 'About a chicken. It wore a patch over its eye like a pirate and a sock on its head. And it was always chasing me. Like it wanted the other sock – only I didn't have it.'

I stared at Ted, who shrugged.

'Dreams can be really weird,' he said.

'This felt different though,' I insisted. 'It was so bright and vivid, like when someone turns up the colours on the TV. And listen, Tinkle was in it. She was lying in this cave and I could see light and an opening high up above. She sounded so sad. And lost. I think she was hurt – one of her wings was lying awkwardly by her side.'

'That really is an awful dream,' Aura said, looking up from the pad of paper in front of her, her pencil poised over the dragon she was drawing.

'But what if it was more than a dream?' I insisted.

'What do you mean?' she asked.

'There are times I've shared dreams with Flicker and he's shown me things. You know, the forest and the volcano.'

'But Flicker wasn't there with you, was he?' Aura said.

I shook my head.

'So it probably is just a dream,' Liam said. 'Nothing to worry about.' He gave a slight shudder. 'Like the chicken.'

'Hold on,' Ted said. 'Did you say you had the

dream while you were tucked up with Lolli?'

I nodded. 'She couldn't sleep because of her arm, so I was telling her a story and we both fell asleep.'

Ted looked thoughtful.

'Perhaps you were sharing *her* dream? Do you remember what you told us your mum said about imprinting?'

I nodded again.

'What if that happens with dragons too? Most of the dragons hatch and fly off before we really get very close. It's the ones we've hatched ourselves that have stuck around.'

'I didn't hatch Zing,' I said, staring up at the little dragon who was perched on my bookshelf.

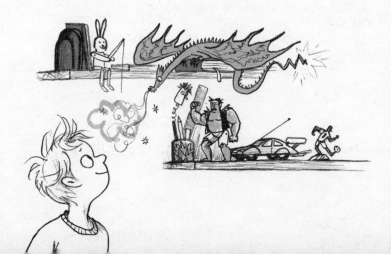

'Not intentionally. But you did tread on his fruit and then he flew at your face,' he said with a little chuckle and then added, 'Yours was definitely the first face he connected with! It makes you think we should probably be a bit more careful not to get too close when they're hatching.'

There was a little squeak, which I realised had come from Aura.

'Sorry,' she said quickly, motioning to the bag next to her. 'Um . . . I caught my finger in the zip.'

'But here's the thing,' Ted went on. 'What if when they imprint on you, you imprint on them too. Let's face it – we're all pretty attached to our dragons, aren't we? So what if Lolli is so attached to Tinkle, she's feeling what Tinkle is feeling.'

I thought of Lolli's sore arm and then pictured Tinkle lying in the cave with her wing at that odd angle.

'You could be right!' I said jumping up. 'And maybe that's why Flicker seemed so sad when I saw him,' I suggested. 'Tinkle is hurt and he doesn't know where she is. I have to let him know. So he can find her and help her. Then Lolli will get better too.'

'But if it's true and Tinkle's really fallen and can't fly back out, how is Flicker knowing where she is going to help them?' Liam asked. 'We need to figure out what to do about her wing first.'

There was a moment's silence.

'Let's ask my mum,' I said quickly. 'I just need to think of a way to ask her without actually letting on what kind of animal we're talking about.'

21
Mum to the Rescue

Downstairs we found Mum getting things ready for another live recording of the TV show – this time, thankfully on location at a local animal sanctuary. Dad had decided to do battle with the garden and was outside wrestling with a reluctant and grumpy lawnmower, which had decided it had better things to do than cut grass.

'Any time you lot fancy helping tame our jungle, just say the word,' Mum said, nodding towards the open back door. 'You probably all have bright green fingers from spending so much time in Grandad's garden.'

I must have grinaced, because she gave a little chuckle.

'Something special about Grandad's garden, hey?' She paused. 'Maybe it's all those caramel toffees and Nana's jam tarts.'

We all smiled and nodded.

'We were wondering if we could ask you something?' I said.

'Your professional opinion,' added Ted seriously.

'Of course,' Mum replied. 'Fire away. Oh dear, you haven't got a problem with your guinea pig, have you, Ted?'

'No, it's not a guinea pig,' I said.

'More of a bird,' Aura put in. 'It belongs to a friend of Mamma's,' she added quickly.

'Oh,' said Mum. 'Well, what seems to be the problem?'

'We think it's hurt its wing,' I said. 'And we just wondered, if it was broken or something, is there anything we could do?'

'Because it might be trapped,' piped up Liam. 'In a really deep hole.'

I glared at him and shook my head. If Mum thought there was a creature in trouble she'd leap straight into animal-saviour mode. She'd be prepping ropes and insisting on abseiling in there to rescue it.

Her eyes widened.

'It's not trapped,' I said quickly. 'Liam got that bit wrong. It's just hurt its wing. And we thought you might know what we could do to help it get better quicker.'

'Hmmm,' Mum said. 'Wings are tricky. First of all, you should make sure the poor thing is somewhere warm and quiet and contained, so it feels safe and doesn't flap about in distress and make any injury worse.'

'Anything else?' I asked.

'Well, if the wing has been bashed but isn't broken, it will just need some time to heal. Like Lolli,' she said with a little smile. 'Sometimes it can just be about waiting.'

'So it could get better on its own?'

'Without actually seeing it, it's impossible to say. Why doesn't she bring it round for me to have a proper look? Maybe I should phone your mum, Aura?'

'No,' I blurted too loudly, making Mum give me a weird look. 'I mean, no, don't worry about that. We'll tell her. We don't want to make you late for your filming.'

Mum headed off, giving me her 'there's something funny going on here you're not telling me' look.

Aura, who was still clutching her rucksack, hissed, 'She might have been more help if she'd known exactly what we were talking about.'

'Well, it's not like she's got a lot of experience of treating dragons,' Liam said.

'True,' Ted said, 'but at least she'd have more information, rather than trying to help us with a fictitious bird who may or may not be stuck in a hole.'

That night I lay in bed determined to focus on what I'd seen in Lolli's dream.

Flicker and I had shared dreams before. He had shown me things. So maybe I could show him too?

If I could fall asleep with the image of Tinkle in the cave in my mind, maybe I could fill my dreams with it and Flicker would see.

I closed my eyes and imagined I was there again in the dark, the rock scraping my skin, and the hot air stifling me. I squirmed under my quilt as the flapping bird started pecking at my insides. Poor Tinkle. I didn't want to be in this place even in my dreams. But I made myself focus. As sleep crept towards me though, other images tiptoed closer.

I saw Aura laughing as she stood covered in dragons, holding one out on her hand to her dad. And Grandad's garden surrounded by a fence that grew higher and higher as I tried to climb in over it.

I woke up in the morning, sweaty and exhausted and more desperate than ever. My dreams had been muddled and full of Liam's pirate chicken and dancing socks and a garden of dragons that I could never climb into. How was Flicker going to make sense of any of that?

I threw off the covers, feeling as if I'd swallowed a wasp and it was now buzzing angrily inside me. First flapping birds and now wasps – at this rate I'd be turning into the Old Woman Who Swallowed a Fly!

22
An Explosion of Green

Later that day, in Grandad's garden, I tried to calm the buzzing wasp inside me by digging up some tangled brambles. Grandad and I worked side by side and it felt good to be there, just the two of us.

Once the ground was clear, I wheeled the barrow over to the compost heap. When I got back I found Grandad staring at the rows of trays in his greenhouse.

'Oh dear,' he said sadly. 'Not much that's prizewinning in here, is there?'

I had to admit he was right. The seedlings he'd been growing were definitely looking tired and shrivelled.

'I told Jim I had it all in hand,' Grandad said. 'But it looks like I should have let him take all this lot over to his fancy polytunnel too.'

I shook my head fiercely. It didn't seem fair for Jim to come in and take over. 'Maybe they need some chocolate,' I suggested feebly, grasping at the limits of my gardening know-how.

Grandad smiled. 'I think they just need a bit more protection than I can give them.' He looked up at the cracked panes of glass in the roof of the greenhouse where the wind rattled through and down at the holes in the floor where some night-time creature had dug its way in to nibble on the tender shoots.

'I can repot them for you,' I said. 'And I can fill in those holes and we can board up that window. I'm sure I can fix this place up. You don't need to let Jim take them.'

Grandad scratched his beard and looked around. 'Right you are, Chipstick. We'd better get started then.'

When Aura came skipping down the garden later,

she found me scrabbling about in the dirt trying to fill in the holes.

Grandad explained about his suffering plants as he poured us all a glass of squash and handed Aura a biscuit.

'It'll be fine once I've fixed the place up,' I said, rubbing the dirt off my hands and grabbing myself a biscuit too, before they all vanished.

'Don't worry,' she said brightly. 'Just leave it to me and Rosebud. I'm sure we can sort things.'

Grandad looked at the little dragon who was clinging to Aura's arm. He reached out a finger and gently tapped her scaly head.

'Well, if you think you can turn things around then, I'd certainly be glad of any help.'

There was a noise like a snort that I suddenly realised might have come from me.

'Any *extra* help, that is,' he corrected himself, glancing at me.

I stuffed another biscuit into my mouth to stop any grumpy words getting out. It was all very well for

Aura to swan in and offer to save the day, but I'd been the one working hard to clear things up.

As Grandad went back to the house for a cuppa and a quiet half-hour, I got back to filling holes. Aura whispered something to Rosebud and the little dragon started hopping from tray to tray, breathing gently across the seedlings. It was like a breath of fresh air filling the greenhouse, and you could almost see each little plant lift its head and smile at the dragon in thanks.

'Come on,' Aura said happily. 'Let's go and have a cup of tea with your nana. Rosebud has got this.'

I watched Rosebud for a moment, rubbing my arm where a nettle had stung me. Maybe it was time for a break. With Rosebud on the job, hopefully Grandad's garden would soon be back to prizewinning status.

But let's face it – a lot can happen in the time it takes to drink some tea. Especially when a dragon has been left in charge.

When we came back, I could tell something was wrong with the greenhouse, even from halfway down the path. There were tendrils shooting out of the broken windows, reaching up into the air. It looked like some bizarre green octopus.

But it wasn't just the greenhouse.

Everywhere we looked, plants had erupted, sending shoots out in all directions. And every single one was covered in tiny buds ready to bloom. It was as if the garden had turned jungle in the blink of an eye.

Grandad just stared. His mouth dropped open as he watched some of the tendrils stretching over towards Jim's neat flower beds and vegetable plot.

And then our eyes fell on his polytunnel.

And the explosion of green that filled it.

Rosebud was flitting back and forth across the gardens, happily breathing life into everything she saw. Which would have been fine if she'd known when to stop.

'What have you done?' I cried. 'Make her stop, Aura!'

Aura raced down the garden, calling to her little

dragon, who ignored her and carried on flying from plant to plant. By the time Grandad and I reached them, Aura's legs were entwined with creeping tendrils and she had flowers sprouting from her hair.

'I was only trying to help,' she wailed. 'I'm so sorry.'

Grandad wrapped one arm round her shoulder and with the other hand he pulled the leafy tendril – that was now covered in snot – off her face.

'There, there,' he said. 'No need for tears.'

23
Follow That Dream

That night, I needed to be asleep and dreaming, to make sure Flicker got the message about Tinkle.

But however many sheep I counted and however still I lay I just couldn't debuzz enough to drift off. After Aura had arrived in the garden and caused chaos, the angry wasp inside me had just got buzzier and buzzier.

Mum and Dad had gone to bed hours ago and it was pitch dark outside. I slumped down in bed while Zing perched on my desk, watching me. And then I saw a flash of light flare across the window. And a low familiar rumble. I leaped out of bed, got my foot caught in the quilt and yelped as I nosedived onto the floor. Rubbing my face, I raced to the window.

Flicker stared in at me and his diamond eyes sent little darts of light straight into my heart. They had an immediately calming effect on the wasp.

But had my message been too garbled for him to understand? Was that why he was here, and not out looking for Tinkle? I took a breath, determined to make my words less muddled than my dreams.

Flicker leaned in closer as if waiting for me to climb on his neck. But I held up a hand and shook my head. There was no time for fun and games. I told him of the dream I'd shared with Lolli in as much detail as I could, my mind filling with images of the cave.

When I told him that the injured dragon was Tinkle and how sad her song had sounded, I had the same fluttery feeling deep in my chest, remembering how scared I had felt in the stifling dark. Flicker's scales flared bright orange. And his body shook as if in sudden readiness to launch up into the air.

I let my hand drop from where it had been stroking his neck. My eyes fell on the pile of paper on my desk. When Aura and the others had been here yesterday, she had drawn the four-winged dragon on sheet after sheet after sheet. The one Elvi always spoke to her about – her mum's dragon.

I so wanted to tell Flicker the rest of what was in my head. How Aura had wanted to tell her dad about the dragons, because she felt so sad about her mum not seeing them. And the secret worries I had about Aura taking over in Grandad's garden. And how afraid I was that there wouldn't be a place for me any more if she did.

All those worries buzzing away inside me, desperate to get out. I ran a finger over the sheets of paper as Flicker leaned in. He sniffed at them and then let out a puff of steam that set them fluttering, lifting the four-winged dragon into the air. But I bit back those worries. There wasn't time now. Flicker needed to go, and fast.

He nudged me with his snout, and I felt the warmth from his scales spread through me.

Then he turned his head and rocketed up into the sky.

24
Superheroes Don't Wear Tea Towels

I don't often oversleep. Mainly because Lolli usually helps me wake up on time by jumping on me, banging a drum near my head or singing at full volume. But with her still cocooned in her nest and me not being able to sleep for ages after Flicker had left, I was out for the count when Mum put her head round the door.

'You feeling OK, Tomas?' she asked.

I peered blearily at her. 'Just tired,' I grunted.

She came over and sat on the edge of my bed.

'Have you been wrestling crocodiles in your sleep again?' she asked, reaching out to pat my tangled hair.

'Sort of,' I said. Because actually thinking about all the things I had in my head felt about as exhausting as wrestling crocodiles sometimes.

Mum leaned in and gave me a squeeze. 'Well, if you need me to talk to those crocs, let me know,' she said.

And I smiled, because as usual Mum had got it without me spelling it out. But just in case I needed to hear it loud and clear, she added, 'I know things have been busy lately with the filming, but I'm always here if you need me.'

I was just about to answer, when Zing started scratching at the underside of my bed.

'Whatever's that?' Mum said.

'Nothing,' I cried, and then started coughing loudly as the scratching became more frenzied.

Mum stood up and began to lean down to look underneath. But I scrambled out of bed, flinging the quilt so it covered her view. I stood between her and the bed, hoping Zing wouldn't do anything more alarming.

She wrinkled her nose and sniffed and I realised

there was a definite whiff of something burning.

'It's the class hamster,' I blurted. 'It's really stinky – that's why no one wants to look after it. So I said I'd do it.'

There was another noise from under the bed, which I could tell was Zing trying to get himself free from the tangle of jumpers he'd dragged under there. Any second now he'd be flaring silver and then zapping goodness knows where. Knowing my luck, onto the top of Mum's head!

Mum eyed me warily. 'I'm not convinced your class hamster sounds very happy under there. Maybe we should find it somewhere else to sleep.'

'Absolutely,' I said quickly. 'I'll sort old Hammy out, don't worry. You go and check on Lolli – I'm an expert hamster whisperer.'

She looked as if she was about to comment on that, but then Dad called out to her.

'Make sure you keep Hammy out of Tomtom's way,' she said to me firmly, before heading out.

I opened the window for Zing, who zipped outside and happily started zig-zagging between the branches of the nearest tree.

I quickly got dressed and then started shoving my school things into my bag. While I did, I gave the seedling my usual hopeful inspection. Since I'd scattered the soil with cacao I'd been keeping a close eye on it. I'd been cautiously optimistic after seeing the leaves turn green again in places. But today it positively shone. I rubbed my eyes just to be sure it wasn't tiredness playing tricks. No. The seedling was bigger and the leaves bright and glossy. And it definitely had a glow!

I punched the air and whooped, bringing Zing zooming back inside to see what the fuss was about.

'Look,' I cried, pointing to the little pot. 'I did it!'

Zing flew down and clung to my jumper and his tail thumped happily on my back.

I couldn't wait until the bell rang at the end of the day so I could go to the botanic garden and share the news with Chouko. Liam and Ted had football practice and Aura, who'd hardly looked in my direction all day, had hurried away for an appointment of some kind. But that didn't matter. I had found the answer and I was going to save those seedlings.

I felt like a superhero swooping in to rescue the day as I raced through the gates of the botanic garden. And as if the stars were lining up in my favour, I spotted

Chouko as soon as I turned the corner.

I waved and called out. But she was too focused on reading whatever was on the clipboard in her hand.

Before I could reach her, a young man in overalls approached and the two of them started talking intently. I hung back, wanting to speak to her alone. But just when I thought they were done another woman joined them. She was wearing a white lab coat and clutching a clipboard. She jumped into the

conversation and started jabbing a finger at whatever was written on the board.

The talking went on and on, with the woman in the lab coat now doing most of it. I couldn't see Chouko's face, but when you watch a person closely you can actually tell all sorts of things even from the back. People aren't aware how much their body does the talking for them, and from the way her shoulders had crept upwards, I could tell Chouko wasn't very happy.

I started jiggling about impatiently. I couldn't help it. Why couldn't they just finish up what they were saying and leave Chouko alone?

When they finally headed off, I ran over.

'Chouko,' I wheezed, out of breath from running.

For once she didn't look pleased to see me.

'Hello, Tomas. I'm sorry I can't stop and talk right now. There's something I need to do. Rather urgently.'

'But I have something important to tell you,' I said quickly. 'About the seedlings and why they're struggling. I know what you can do to help them.'

She frowned slightly and looked thoughtful. 'Yes, well, they've been taken out of my hands – for the time being anyway.' She looked in the direction the woman had left and frowned again. 'Though we shall see about that.'

'What do you mean?' I asked, alarmed. 'Who's taken them?'

'The department are very interested in my research. But apparently *some* people feel that I am not equipped to look after the seedlings adequately.' She gave a little snort and I saw her knuckles whiten around the coffee cup she was holding. 'So,' she continued, 'my specimens have been moved temporarily into a more intensively monitored area of the department. Into one of the laboratories over there.' She waved a hand towards the building in the distance. 'And apparently they are to stay there until Dr Meadows decides if anything further is required.'

I stared at her. The words were crashing around in my head and I wanted to shout at them to sit down and be quiet so I could think straight.

'But I have to see them,' I blurted at last. 'I know what they need. It's –' But she cut me off before I could get the word out.

'I'm sorry, Tomas, no one is allowed in there. They are operating under closed conditions. I'm still trying to convince them to give *me* access.'

I opened my mouth to plead, but she laid a hand on my arm and said gently, 'I'm sorry, Tomas. I really have to go.'

And so there I was, left on the path, feeling like I'd just been told my superhero cape was in fact a damp tea towel.

25
The Best Defence

The next morning before I went down for breakfast I popped my head into Lolli's room. She was curled up in her nest fast asleep, making an occasional snuffling sound like a contented guinea pig.

'Think I'll let her sleep,' Dad said coming up the stairs. 'She was awake for hours last night, poor Lolli. Getting herself all worked up.'

He peered over to look at her. 'Looks pretty peaceful now, thank goodness.'

It was a relief to see Lolli sleeping more comfortably. I just hoped it meant that Flicker had found Tinkle and that she was feeling more comfortable too. Or then again, maybe they had just exhausted themselves?

On the way to school, I kept thinking about the seedlings at the botanic garden and how they were being monitored. A toxic mix of alarm and frustration rose up in me. Why couldn't Chouko have just listened to what I had to say?

When I got to school I found Liam and Ted outside class, talking to Mr Peters about the upcoming football tournament and the extra practice at lunchtime. There was no sign of Aura.

Mr Firth strode in and started herding everyone inside.

'But it's Friday, sir. We have Miss Jelinski on a Friday,' Amira said brightly, as if our teacher might have forgotten what day he was striding through.

Mr Firth stopped and turned to look at her.

'Yes, Amira, I'm well aware that it is indeed Friday. Miss Jelinski is unwell today, so you have the pleasure of *my* company again.'

As we took our seats, he began blaring out instructions.

'Take our your science books,' he bellowed, as if we were several miles away across a windswept desert. 'Today we're looking at how animals defend themselves. Who can give me an example?'

He glared at Mahid, who was whispering to Seb. Seb noticed the predator closing in on them and quickly elbowed Mahid, then shrank back into his chair.

Make yourself small, I thought. That's one defence.

'Er . . . hedgehogs,' Mahid stammered.

Mr Firth grunted, clearly displeased that Mahid had actually still been listening, though to be fair most of this hemisphere would have had a hard job blocking out Mr Firth's bellows. Mahid looked as if he wanted to turn hedgehog himself and curl up in a ball under the ferocious glare being fixed on him. I pictured him rolling up and his spines poking Mr Firth in the nose.

'Skunks use their disgusting stink,' Ted ventured.

'And sea urchins are prickly,' said Lila. 'I know cos my little brother touched one last summer and he totally screamed forever about it. And then Dad said he couldn't have an ice cream and he screamed even louder. Actually, maybe that was why he was screaming in the first place. Anyway it was really prickly and . . .'

Mr Firth blew out a sigh that rattled the window panes. 'Yes, that's enough, thank you, Lila. But you're right that there are many sea creatures that defend themselves in a multitude of ways. Take the cuttlefish for example. They can produce bands of colour. It acts like a mesmerising light show that lulls its prey into a trance.'

Mr Firth tapped his laptop and a photo popped up on the whiteboard.

Ted was leaning forward in rapt attention – this sort of lesson was right up his street, and I could see he was bursting to tell Mr Firth one of his own amazing facts – but at that moment the door creaked open and Aura appeared, quickly apologising for being late. I'm surprised she didn't crumple to the floor from the look Mr Firth gave her. He tutted loudly as she walked to her seat, leaving a trail of muddy footprints on the carpet.

'You'll be staying in at break to clear that up,' he grumbled.

She slid into the chair next to me and I noticed her hands were covered in dirt like her shoes.

'I forgot it'd take a bit longer to get to school from your grandparents',' she whispered.

I was taken aback. 'You've been there this morning?'

'Of course,' she replied. 'I've been helping your grandad clear up.'

'Oh,' I said. 'I was planning to go round after school to help.'

'It's not really your responsibility,' she replied. 'I should do it.'

I stared blankly at her. Not my responsibility? What did she mean? The angry wasp inside me woke up, gave a buzz and started knocking against the jam jar of my chest.

'Then again, I can't go back till tomorrow. I've got another eye test after school. They think I need glasses. So maybe it would be good if you do go.'

Before I could say anything more, I realised Mr Firth had stopped talking and was glowering at both of us, his finger pointing at Aura.

'Late and now disruptive. I think perhaps you

175

should stay in at lunch as well as break, Aura. Now be quiet and open your book.'

I stared down at the page in front of me, my mind so distracted that the words squatted sourly on the paper, refusing to leap up and be read.

Since when was Grandad's garden Aura's responsibility?

26
Stuck in the Mud

After a whole day with Mr Firth I felt limper than a soggy piece of lettuce. I hadn't even had anyone to distract me at lunchtime, with Ted and Liam at football and Aura kept inside. Still, I wasn't going to let any of that stop me helping Grandad. As I came down the garden after school I could see he and Aura had already made good progress. But there was still plenty to do.

'Where's the wheelbarrow?' I asked as Grandad handed me a spade.

'Just behind the dragon-fruit tree,' he replied. 'I

think Aura was clearing a patch over there earlier. She did a great job this morning.'

I stared over at the tree, imagining Aura there, and suddenly felt as if some creepy-crawly with a million legs was scuttling down my back. I dug my spade into a patch of nettles that were in full flower, thanks to Rosebud's breath, and spent the next half an hour digging, my thoughts churning as I churned the mud. With every thought the spade got heavier, until I was grunting in frustration.

Eventually Grandad, who'd been whistling one of his tunes that couldn't quite make up its mind what to be, paused.

'You OK, Chipstick? Trying to dig your way to Australia?' He chuckled, but then turned serious when my shoulders sagged.

'Anything you want to chat about?' he asked gently.

I grunted something that turned out to be more huff than words.

'Oh dear. One of those days, is it?'

I sighed and nodded.

'Well, first off, how about you get yourself out of that there mud? Can't think straight when you're stuck in a muddy hole.'

I looked down at my wellies. The soles were heavy with clods of thick wet earth.

I let out a groan and tried to shake one clean. But it was sticky stuff and when I lifted the other one, my foot just sank even deeper.

'You actually need to take a step out of it,' Grandad said with an encouraging smile. 'No good noticing what's wrong and then carrying on stamping up and down in it.'

I took a stride towards him, feeling the cloggy weight of my boots.

'There now, give them a bash and a scrape while you chew on one of these.' And he popped a caramel toffee into my mouth. It interrupted my frown and I bit down, ready to taste the creamy toffee. But my taste buds did a little jump in surprise.

'What flavour's that?' I asked through sticky teeth.

'You tell me,' he said.

I rolled the toffee around my mouth, trying to unravel the taste exploding on my tongue. It was sweet, but also a bit like . . .

'It's salty,' I declared. I wasn't sure whether I liked it or not. I chewed for a bit longer, trying to decide. A butterfly fluttered down and settled on the handle of Grandad's spade.

He watched it, smiling.

'Good job we took a breather,' he said. 'Else this little fella wouldn't have had anywhere to rest up.'

Its wings were smoky blue bordered by white, and its antennae twitched as it looked around. I carried on chewing my toffee as I watched it, absent-mindedly stomping my feet.

'Looks like you're all unstuck,' said Grandad.

And the twinkle in his eye made me think that it probably wasn't just the mud he was talking about. I realised that my thoughts had finally stopped churning.

Inside my head it felt like a fresh gentle breeze had started to blow, clearing the skies and letting me think clearly again.

'Can I have another one of those toffees?'

'Anytime you like,' he said with a wink.

'So how did Jim take the sudden growth spurt in his garden?' I asked as I unwrapped the sweet. 'He hasn't tried to take over again, has he?'

Grandad held up a hand as he paused to wait for a sneeze. It tickled across his face until it erupted out in an explosive *aatishoo!* that rattled the bean poles.

'No, course not. He's only trying to help,' he said. 'Truth be told, I think he's a bit worried we've taken on more than we could handle. He might be right too.'

He bent and picked up one of the tendrils that had bloomed thanks to Rosebud's breath. Pink and yellow petals spilled over his arm.

'You know Jim – he likes a good moan. But he came round soon enough. Especially once he saw some of these flowers. Thanks to that little dragon Jim now thinks I've got the greenest fingers around.'

He leaned towards me and rescued a beetle that had been crawling up my sleeve.

'Don't look so surprised,' he added. 'I know it wasn't exactly what we asked for, but in among all that tangle of tendrils there are some really lovely flowers. Where is Aura anyway?' he added, looking about in case she might suddenly appear from behind a bush.

When I didn't reply, he stopped and peered at me as if my thoughts might helpfully be written in ink across my face.

'You know she was just trying to help too, don't you, Chipstick?' he said at last.

I gave a little shrug. But I knew that wasn't going to work with Grandad. He'd stand there and wait for as long as it took for me to spill the beans.

I swallowed the last mouthful of toffee and then said simply, 'Aura is Elvi's granddaughter.'

Grandad's eyebrows leaped up his forehead like fuzzy caterpillars doing the high jump.

'She was growing dragons before I even knew about the tree,' I added.

The fuzzy caterpillars didn't come down Grandad's forehead until I'd finished telling him the whole story of how we'd found out who Aura was.

'Well, that must have been a bit of a shock,' he said.

'Just a bit!' I spluttered.

'For both of you,' he added. 'Aura's had a lot to take on all at once, what with starting a new school too. How did she take it?'

I was a bit surprised by his question. After all, I was the one that was having problems getting my head round this. 'She's fine,' I said.

Grandad nodded but didn't say anything.

'Kat says Aura isn't going to think the tree belongs to her,' I said desperately. 'But what if she does?'

Grandad sniffed in a deep breath of air and smiled. 'Smart kid, that Kat. She's right – the dragon-fruit tree is under our care, but it doesn't belong to anyone. Aura knows that. She's not trying to take over, Chipstick.

183

She just feels bad for causing so much mess.'

'How can you be so sure?'

He reached into his pocket, pulled out a folded piece of paper and handed it to me to read. It was a letter from Aura. An apology.

'I told her she needn't fret, but she said she was responsible and it was up to her to sort everything out.'

I bit the corner of my lip.

'She told me that too,' I said. 'Only I thought she meant something different. I thought she meant that the dragons were her responsibility. And I wasn't needed any more.'

Grandad gave a little chuckle. 'I can see how that might have set off a few alarm bells in your head,' he said, ruffling my hair.

I gave a sheepish smile. Was Grandad right? Had it all been in my head? Now I thought about it, I had to admit that Aura hadn't done anything to make me think she had some master plan to take over the dragons. She was a bit loud and annoying sometimes, but she'd also looked after Lolli, giving her that picture when she heard she was hurt. And we'd always had fun with the dragons – together.

Grandad nodded at the garden. 'Look around, Chipstick – all these flowers blooming.'

I took it all in. It really was a riot of colour in the garden right now.

'It might be a bit of a mess, and more chaotic than you'd like it to be, but see all those new buds, all that possibility waiting to burst out. We wouldn't have any of that without Aura.'

I watched as he lifted his arm and the breeze blew a handful of bright red petals into the air, scattering them in all directions.

He grinned at me and winked. 'I reckon Aura's a bit like these, don't you? A bright, chaotic burst of new life in the garden. And that's not so bad now, is it?'

I thought about it for a minute. 'No,' I said slowly. 'I guess, it's not.'

'Don't you forget,' he added, 'this garden – and those dragons – need the both of you. There's no question about that.'

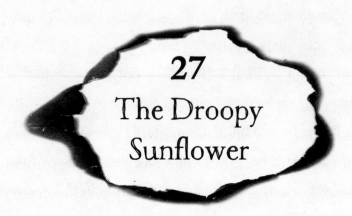

27
The Droopy Sunflower

Grandad was right, the dragons did need us. They needed us all, working together. I knew I had to patch things up with Aura, let her know the chaos in Grandad's garden wasn't her fault and that I wasn't blaming her.

The seedlings needed us too. If Chouko wasn't going to listen to me, we had to take matters into our own hands and get to them ourselves. We had to sprinkle them with cacao and keep them healthy. Until we figured out how to rescue them.

I met Liam outside Ted's house, and when we got inside and hurried up to his room I saw Aura was already there. I tried to catch her eye to smile, but she was fiddling with the rucksack on her lap and didn't look up.

Thanks to Grandad helping to clear my head of the tangle of worries, there was a lot more room for ideas. In fact, my brain was back to churning new ones out rather than just churning a few old ones round and round. Everything from finding another driller dragon to tunnel our way to the seedlings, to abseiling off the back of a dragon into the building.

'Brilliant,' said Liam. 'And we could get Kai to send Dodger over,' he went on. 'With his cloaking skills, we could get really close and no one would even see us.'

'That's all well and good,' Ted said, 'but we have to find them first. They could be anywhere inside those laboratories. You said not even Chouko knows exactly where they are. We have to locate them and then check the plan will work. No point using a driller dragon if they're up on the top floor!'

Ted was right. In my excitement at coming up with a grand plan I'd missed a critical step. Finding the seedlings. And if Chouko couldn't get near them, what hope did we have?

'We need brain food,' Ted said. 'Come on, Liam, let's go for supplies.'

While Ted and Liam went downstairs to raid the kitchen, I looked over at Aura. She'd kept very quiet all through the wild planning stages. It felt like when Lolli's quiet because she's hurt, and I didn't like it one bit.

I stuck out a hand for Rosebud to come and perch on. The little dragon flew over and then bobbed her head up and down, folding back her wings as she made herself comfy.

'It's good we have Rosebud,' I said. 'If anyone spots us, we can send her in to fart on them – they'll be too busy giggling their way through her green gases to take any notice of us.'

Aura gave a feeble smile. She was sitting cross-legged by Ted's bed, one hand clutching Elvi's diary, the other still wrapped around her bag. She stared at Rosebud as she hopped across the carpet. With the others gone, I knew now was the time to try and fix things.

My worries about the garden belonging to her before had run wild lately and taken over completely. Looking at her now, with the tangle of those worries cleared away, I could see she looked like a sunflower that no one had watered. All droopy.

'So what do you think?' I said. 'You're always great at plans.'

'I'm not,' she said quickly. Then she muttered, 'They always end up getting us in more trouble. You're better off without my stupid ideas.'

'That's not true,' I said – even though until my chat with Grandad I'd probably have agreed with her.

'It is,' she insisted miserably.

She hugged her bag closer to her chest, like I did with Pink Dog when I was worried.

'Listen,' I said seriously, 'you know Grandad is fine about what happened with Rosebud in the garden, don't you?' I paused and then added, 'It wasn't your fault.'

She looked up, and her eyes went a bit shiny.

'Thanks, Tomas.' Then she sniffed and said, 'But I feel terrible. I was trying to help and I just made a huge mess. I couldn't stop Rosebud.'

Her hand stroked the diary. 'I'm supposed to know what I'm doing. Elvi was my amma and she knew everything about the dragons. I wanted to make her proud,' she said at last. 'You always seem to know what you're doing – just like her.'

I couldn't help laughing. 'I really don't,' I said. 'And I'm not sure Elvi did all the time either.'

'I bet she knew not to let a swarm of bee dragons imprint on her,' Aura said fiercely.

28
Plan Bee

'Hang on, what are you talking about?' I asked.

I watched as Aura put her finger to her lips and carefully unzipped the bag a little. I leaned forward to peer inside.

It was full of the tiny multicoloured dragons that had flown out of the dragon-fruit tree earlier that week. I gazed in at the mass of bright colours and glittering orange wings.

'The first dozen or so flew straight off. But these were the ones that landed on me, and they all stowed away in my bag. When Ted started talking about imprinting, I realised that's what must have happened. You think one dragon makes a mess, you should try living with thirty-seven!'

Her voice must have startled the little dragons because the bag suddenly became a whirl of colour and wings. And then the dragons burst out, making us both jump back in surprise.

Aura looked at me nervously. 'I didn't know what to do, Tomas. It's a good job Dad's been so busy the last few days. At least Mum can't see them.'

'Why didn't you tell me?' I said.

'I thought you'd be cross,' Aura replied. 'That you'd think I'd hatched them on purpose because I wanted more dragons or something. I mean, it's your tree after all.'

It suddenly made a lot more sense why Aura had been avoiding me lately. She hadn't been plotting some big takeover at all.

I sank back against the bed and looked up at the dragons now whizzing round Ted's room.

'It's not my tree,' I said gently. 'And the dragons certainly don't belong to anyone. To be fair, any one of us would have struggled to live with thirty-seven of them.'

I ducked as a line of the bee dragons shot down towards my head.

'How did you even get them in that bag?' I asked.

'Oh, that's easy,' she said. 'Honey.' And she took a jar out from the bag, opened it and dribbled some of the golden honey onto the lid. Immediately the dragons flew down and clustered around it.

'Looks like you know more than you think you do about dragons,' I said, relieved that we weren't going to have to catch the tiny creatures.

'That was just luck,' she said. 'I was eating breakfast and they wouldn't leave my toast alone.'

'But that's all we ever do,' I said. 'Figure things out as we go along. And make mistakes,' I added.

'Well, I make a lot of those,' she said. And I noticed again how deflated she looked.

'But you're always so confident and . . . you know . . .'

'Loud?' she said, finishing the sentence for me.

I gave a small grin. 'A bit, yeah. I mean you did sweep into school like a mini-tornado.'

'You try joining a school halfway through Year Six,' she said with a shrug. 'Anyway, being loud doesn't necessarily mean you feel confident.'

I thought about what Grandad had said, how Aura had had a lot to get used to. First, joining a new class and making new friends, and then immediately having to say goodbye to Kat, who she had got on so well with. And then finding out about the dragons, Elvi growing them, *and* the weirdness about her mum not seeing them. It really was a lot to take in.

I pointed at Rosebud, who had curled up on Aura's arm, her petal-like wings folded over and her head tucked inside.

'She must trust you a lot to do that,' I said, and then I added firmly, 'and she's right to.'

Aura looked down at Rosebud and touched a wing with one fingertip. The petal opened and Rosebud's little head peeked out and sniffed at Aura before going straight back to sleep. She smiled. 'Thanks, Tomas.'

Zing, who'd been happily charging himself up by rolling around in a nest of jumpers was flaring silver. As the door opened and Ted entered with a huge container of popcorn, the dragon disappeared in a zap and reappeared right in front of his face. Ted yelped in surprise and flung the popcorn in the air. It rained down on Liam, who'd stepped in behind him with a packet of jam tarts. These went flying too. Two splatted on the carpet, one landed on Ted's upturned face and the other was intercepted by Zing.

He darted away with the tart stuck fast, the little silver-foil case on his back like a turtle's shell.

'I know they're not as good as your nana's,' Ted said, wiping the jam off his face and giving it a lick, 'but they're not too bad at all.'

I started scraping up the sticky splats while Liam scooped up popcorn.

'Thanks for that,' I said, rolling my eyes at Zing. But he'd zipped away already and had appeared on the windowsill outside.

He strutted up and down with the tin foil case on his back, his head tipping back every so often to nibble at the pastry.

'I sometimes forget he doesn't need a door or a window,' Liam said.

'No,' I said. 'He's lucky he can just zap in and out as he pleases.'

And then Ted suddenly piped up. 'Hang on – that's it. We can send Zing in. *He* can find the seedlings.'

'Of course!' I said.

Aura jumped up, a glittery ring of bee dragons circling her. 'And then what if Zing showed this lot the way? We wouldn't need to get ourselves in at all. They can do what bees do, buzzing from plant to plant, but rather than pollinating they'll be fertilising them for us.'

'Yes!' Ted grinned. 'With chocolate!'

'That's brilliant!' I cried.

Aura's face broke into a huge grin. And suddenly it was like the sunflower had found the sunlight again.

29
Twirly Twirly

I slept soundly, my dreams far more peaceful than they'd been for days. When I found myself in the cave again, staring down at Tinkle curled up, her wing still cradled by her side, I felt calmer. This time she seemed to see me. Her eyes stared into mine and her song, which had lost its sadness, filled the air. I sang with her. And in our song was all the brightness of the stars and the colours of the aurora and the magic of the dragons.

Zing though had clearly not slept quite so well. I could tell this partly by the state of my room – the shredded comic, demolished Lego model, claw marks all over my desk and the huge heap of clothes he'd dragged under my bed. And partly by my hair, which was sticking out in every direction and thanks to all the static charge was refusing to be tamed. Maybe the bee dragons had got him all overexcited with their aerial antics.

Whatever the reason, the last time Zing had revved up this much, most of the electrics in our house had blown. Since I could hear Dad's music playing, I hoped we'd got away with it this time.

But I didn't fancy getting a shock turning on the light or the toaster, so I decided to play it safe and wear a pair of bright yellow washing-up gloves until my hair calmed down.

I guess I must have looked a bit odd sitting at the breakfast table – what with the hair and the gloves. And especially as all the static meant I'd attracted a fair amount of fluff on my way.

'You're very hairy,' Lolli said as she licked the honey and jam and hundreds and thousands off her bread.

It was good to see her up and beetling about again, but I did wonder if Mum and Dad realised this was what she'd make when they said she could get herself some breakfast.

'What's with all the toilet roll?' I asked. She must have used a whole roll at least, wrapping it round and round her arm and shoulder.

'Poorly arm,' she said, though quite happily waving it about.

Mum wandered in then, carrying a towel, which she was inspecting. I noticed the black mark all across it. I guessed that Zing had got into the airing cupboard again. Mum glanced over and took in the scene: sticky-out hair, bright yellow gloves, unravelled toilet roll across the breakfast table.

I decided the best course of action was distraction, so launched into a hundred mile an hour debrief of my latest spelling test.

Mum waited for me to finish.

'You're ever so twirly, Tomas,' she said.

'Twirly, twirly, twirly,' Lolli giggled, getting up and spinning round so that she made the toilet roll fly out around her.

'Are you really OK?' Mum asked me.

'Absolutely,' I said, although the squeak didn't sound as reassuring as I'd hoped.

Mum joined us at the table, pulling the toilet roll

off a piece of jammy bread and eyeing my hairy clothes.

'How's that bird?' she asked. 'The one with the hurt wing.'

I looked over at Lolli. She definitely seemed happier, even though she'd wrapped her arm in padding. I wasn't sure Flicker would be able to do much about a damaged wing. But I hoped a happier Lolli – and my dream – meant that he'd at least found Tinkle.

'We haven't really done anything to fix it,' I said. 'But I think it's perked up a bit. I hope so anyway.'

'Well, that's good to hear,' Mum said. 'Sometimes just being there and making the animal feel safe and comfortable can be all that's needed. Gives the healing a helping hand.'

I smiled. I liked that idea. And again I hoped that somewhere Flicker was tucked up next to Tinkle, helping her to feel better.

'It definitely seemed to work with Lolli,' Mum said, smiling. 'Don't think I didn't notice you sneaking in to keep an eye on her.'

Lolli flapped her way over to me and gave me a sticky kiss.

'Funny thing though,' Mum said, 'Aura's mum didn't know anything about a friend with an injured bird when I asked her about it.'

I took a massive bite of my toast and then motioned to show I couldn't possibly talk through my full mouth. It gave me a few seconds to think. But when I couldn't come up with anything to say, I just stuffed more toast in, until Dad arrived and told Mum it was time to leave for the radio station.

30
Giggling in the Garden

For the rest of the day I watched the clock, counting down the minutes until the superhero squad arrived. All I could think about was the seedlings and how badly they needed us. It was our job to protect them as much as the dragons, and I just hoped we could do it. The weight of responsibility was starting to sit pretty heavily on me, leaving me feeling a bit like a squashed raisin on the bottom of a shoe.

When the time finally came and we set off together, I felt their excited chatter pumping me up again, like air in a tyre. I'd had visions of us commando-crawling our way past the girl at the entrance kiosk, but actually we were in luck. A cluster of families were milling about chatting, while their kids rushed round playing tag. It was easy enough to blend in and then one by one make a dash, past the kiosk window and into the bushes.

With the garden closing, we couldn't just saunter along the main paths, so we threaded our way through the tall bamboo, jumped across the giant stepping stones on the pond and scrambled over the rocks with the heathers and moss.

There was a tree with gnarly branches that draped over the rocks, and we scurried into its embrace, peeking out to check for any stragglers wandering to the exits.

We crouched there, panting, grinning at each other, before we all jumped a mile in shock when a bell suddenly sounded just the other side of the tree.

We froze as a man on a bike came into view, ringing a hand bell.

'Garden's closing,' he hollered.

The sudden yell startled Rosebud so much she farted, and for the next couple of minutes we desperately clamped our hands over our mouths to stop ourselves erupting into loud snorts of laughter.

What made it worse was that the man got off his bike and started fiddling with his phone and headphones when he was only a metre away from us. Poor Ted's eyes were streaming as he stifled his hysterics. I just hoped Zing, who was already revved up with excitement, didn't start unleashing any lightning bolts!

When the gas finally cleared, we still had trouble pulling ourselves together and it was pretty clear we were all a little tightly wound.

'Let's wait here a bit longer,' Aura said. 'Just in case people in the offices and labs are working late.'

'Do you think they have security guards?' Liam asked.

'I doubt it,' Ted said. 'It's not like it's a bank or a shop. There's nothing valuable here.'

'Apart from the last remaining active dragon-fruit trees,' I said ruefully.

'Well, yeah, but luckily for us no one else knows that, do they?' he said. 'And I doubt anyone would bother breaking in to steal a few flowers.'

'Maybe we should be trying to break the seedlings out of there,' Liam suggested. 'Rather than just trying to cover them in chocolate. I mean, if they really are being monitored that closely, what happens if they start glowing? That's going to raise some eyebrows, isn't it?'

'We've been over this,' Aura said quickly. 'We don't want to leave them here any longer than we have to. But stage one is just to get them healthy again. And tiny bee dragons are going to have a much easier time sneaking in than us lot. Then we can move to stage two, convincing Chouko we really do know what they need and insisting she find a way to take them back into her care.'

'There are too many for us to carry off anyway,' I said. 'There were trays and trays of them in her greenhouse, and who knows how many more she found since then. We need an insider's help. Aura's right,' I added. 'For now we have to find out where they are and get that chocolate on them.'

'OK,' Liam said. 'Looks like we'd better get Zing zapping then!'

'Hey, Ted,' Aura sniggered. 'You know we're supposed to be covering the seedlings in chocolate, not ourselves.'

Ted, who had been happily munching his way through a gigantic bar of chocolate, grinned sheepishly.

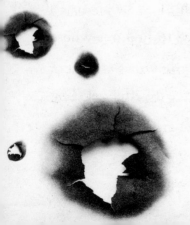

31
Zing Gets Zapping

'This place is huge,' Ted whispered as we huddled in the bushes across the path from the main building. 'I thought gardeners had little sheds and greenhouses, not great big office blocks.'

'Chouko said she's been here since she was a student. I think they have a teaching bit and a research bit and, I don't know, an officey bit, I suppose.'

The truth was, I was just as surprised as the rest of them at exactly how big the building was. I'd only ever been into the cafe that was tucked in at the front of it.

And I'd always been too focused on their home-made ice cream and giant scones to take much notice of the boring-looking offices behind.

There were still a few lights on, and we could see shapes moving in one of the rooms.

'Don't these people have homes to go to?' Liam huffed. 'It's the weekend after all.' We hung back in the shadows and waited. Eventually the lights went out and a few minutes later a group of students left through the side door, locking it behind them.

'OK,' I whispered to Zing, who was clinging to my back. 'It's time.'

I felt his claws dig in as he clambered up a little higher. He leaned out over my shoulder and rubbed his scaly head against my cheek. He'd been swishing his tail back and forth across my jumper for a while, and I could already see the silver threads flaring brightly. I took a handful of batteries out of my pocket and immediately felt his excitement buzzing through me.

'We'd better get you charged up,' I said, placing

them on the ground. 'I don't know how many rooms you'll have to zap in and out before you find them.'

He fluttered down onto the batteries and his sapphire eye sparkled as the batteries gave up their energy. Then his cloudy eye began to swirl and we all stepped back. The next second there was a flash of light, a metallic tang in the air and the little dragon had disappeared.

'Wish he could teleport one of us like that,' Liam said with a laugh.

'I just hope he doesn't run out of charge and get stuck in there,' I said quietly.

For the next ten minutes we stood, eyes fixed on the building. But there was no sign of Zing. Another ten minutes passed, and when he still hadn't reappeared I started to fear the worst.

'What are we going to do?' Ted hissed. 'We can't leave him in there.'

'Maybe he just got bored and zapped off somewhere else?' Liam suggested.

I shook my head. I knew Zing wouldn't stop until he found the seedlings, and if he hadn't reappeared to show the bee dragons the way, then something was definitely wrong.

'I'm going to look for a way in,' I said. I went right up to the building and on tiptoe I peered in through one of the windows on the ground floor. It just looked like an office and I moved along to the next window. This looked more like a science lab, with microscopes on long counters and glass dishes and rows of plants lined up against the wall. But these plants had big round glossy leaves and delicate pink flowers.

As I peered into the last window the others joined me.

'I need to get up there and look in,' I said, pointing to the first floor. 'Maybe he's just lost his bearings.'

'I know I've had a growth spurt,' Ted said, 'but I don't think even I could give you a leg up that high.'

And then a blinding flash of light came from inside one of the windows further along and there was Zing above our heads. Sparks crackled from his silver scales, his tail thrashed from side to side and his eyes stared down at us, fiercely bright.

'What is it?' I cried. 'What's wrong?'

He shot down and grabbed onto my sweatshirt and I jumped at the electric shock that shot through me. But he didn't let go. In fact, his claws tightened on me.

'Ow!' I yelped. And then I watched as Aura's eyes grew wide.

'Tomas . . .' she began.

But I didn't hear the rest, because the next second it felt as if all the atoms of my body had exploded.

When I opened my eyes it was pitch dark. I stumbled forward and crashed into what felt like metal shelving. Something heavy landed on my foot, making me cry out. And then Zing's claws dug in tight again and my atoms exploded once more.

This time I couldn't tell if it was light or dark. Because I was too busy whimpering and clenching my eyes shut. Whatever this was, I didn't like it one little bit. I could feel my heart hammering away in my chest, and when I tried to say something the words just dribbled out my mouth like runny jelly.

'Whadajushappa,' I blubbered.

Slowly I opened my eyes. Zing had let go of my back and was hovering in front of me, his eyes scanning my face. Like he was checking everything was where it should be.

I patted myself down and reassured myself that, yes, my nose was in its proper place.

'Did you just zap me in here with you?' I stammered, looking around.

Zing ignored the question and flew off to the other side of the room.

I followed, my legs not really working properly so I had to stagger along, propping myself up on the countertops.

When I reached him I juddered to a stop. I stared at the sight in front of me, clamping a hand to my mouth in horror.

Nothing could have prepared me for what I saw.

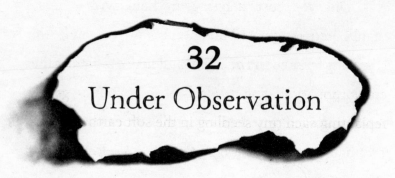

32
Under Observation

Along the counter there were ordered rows of dragon-fruit seedlings in their little pots. Chouko was right, they didn't look healthy any more. But however sad they looked, it was nothing compared to what lay in front of them.

A handful of seedlings had been pinned out on boards. Their straggly roots and tender shoots were gripped tight by metal pins, like when you see beautiful butterflies pinned out on display in those glass cases in museums. A white-hot anger rocketed through me, and I clenched my fists as if that could stop me from blasting off in fury.

'What are they *doing* to you?' I said.

I quickly yanked out the pins, freeing the seedlings from their tiny chains. Then I grabbed some empty pots, scooping handfuls of soil in before gently replanting each tiny seedling in the soft earth.

'You hang in there,' I whispered to them. I thought of the cacao in Aura's bag and wished I had it with me. I rootled in my pocket and found the remains of some that I'd used on the seedling at home. I sprinkled it on the soil. It wasn't much but it was all I had, and I just hoped it would buy us some time.

I spotted a pile of papers and flicked through, my eyes scanning the information. It was clear the seedlings were being closely monitored. One note mentioned 'a strange previously undocumented bioluminescence'. Whoever had been studying them was trying to find out what made them glow.

'We need to get them out of here,' I said to Zing desperately.

Zing's scales had returned to their usual light blue and the silver threads were faint now. I didn't exactly fancy another atom-busting zap out of the building, but I had survived the first time and I couldn't get myself through locked doors any other way.

I looked around the room for something we could use to charge Zing up and spotted the overhead strip lighting. That ought to do it. I pointed to it and Zing fluttered over and tapped the bulb with his tail. The light flared into life and his silver threads flared along with it. I watched him getting brighter and brighter and then braced myself as he flew down towards me.

The room in front of me disappeared and the next moment I was toppling forward into a startled Ted, as Zing and I zapped back into the group.

'OK, what just happened?' Liam spluttered.

I dribbled out an explanation, but not surprisingly they just stared at me, not understanding. Their eyes darted between me, Zing and the windows above.

'I think . . .' Aura said, starting to grin, 'I *think* Zing just teleported Tomas in and out of that building.'

I nodded shakily.

'That is epic!' Ted said.

'I want a go!' cried Liam.

I shook my head. 'You really don't,' I said. It *felt* as if every cell in my body had hurtled down a roller coaster and been flung off into space at the other end and now they were all speeding back towards each other, only some had ended up in the wrong place and were ferociously elbowing their way back into position.

'It hurts,' I said.

I also wasn't sure it was that great for Zing. He had curled up on the ground, his wings lying limply across the grass. He looked exhausted.

'We have to find Chouko right now and tell her what's going on.'

And I quickly explained what I'd seen. Only before I'd completely finished, Aura suddenly grabbed me and pushed me into the bushes, where Liam and Ted stood half hidden. She pressed her finger to her lips and glared at us as a beam of torchlight was cast over the path.

Footsteps came closer and we heard voices. My ears pricked up as I heard the woman I'd seen talking at Chouko last time I was here.

'I have to have those seedlings transferred to my laboratory tonight,' she was saying crossly. 'They need to be in a carefully controlled environment where I can study them properly. Good heavens, man – the way they're looking right now, they could all be dead if we leave them here a moment longer. They could have properties that are revolutionary for science and medicine. Do you really want to be the one responsible for getting in the way of that?'

I stared at Aura in horror, willing the man to argue with her. But he just let out a little defeated sigh and followed her as she hurried along the path.

'Quickly,' I said. 'We have to stop them.'

'How are we supposed to do that?' Liam said.

'We have dragons,' Aura said, her head shrouded in a swirling cloud of bee dragons. 'They'll help us stall them – at least while you go and find Chouko, Tomas. Tell her what you saw and get her to come quick.'

I nodded. She was right. Chouko was our only hope now.

'Look after Zing for me,' I said, scooping him up and handing him to Aura.

'Right,' I heard Ted say to her as I hurried away, 'tell me you've got a plan.'

33
No Joke

I raced down the path to Chouko's cottage and banged on her front door.

'Chouko!' I yelled. 'Please, we need you.'

I peered through the letter box. But there was no sign of her inside. I hurried round to the greenhouses, but she wasn't in there either.

I called her name again, desperation turning my voice all squeaky. And then I saw her head pop up from a bush further down the garden and sprinted towards her.

'Tomas? What are you doing here?' she asked.

'The garden's closed. Oh dear, you haven't got yourself locked in, have you?'

'No,' I said breathlessly. 'We need you to come quickly. They're taking the seedlings. And you have to stop them.'

Chouko gave a sigh. Shaking her head, she picked up the handles of the wheelbarrow. 'I don't know why you're so interested in these particular seedlings. I've tried my best, Tomas. Obviously I don't appreciate other people swooping in and taking over my research, but I'm not sure there's anything more I can do. But you mustn't worry – I'm sure they will be well looked after.'

'They won't,' I insisted. 'I've seen what they've done to them in there.'

Chouko frowned. 'I hope you haven't been wandering off the proper paths again, Tomas? Exploring where you shouldn't be.'

I shook my head. There wasn't time for this. 'Please, Chouko. They're not looking after them at all,' I wailed. 'They don't even know how.'

'That's why they are so keen to study them, to see if they can understand what we are doing wrong.'

'But they're going to end up killing them. They're trying to find out what's so special about them. But I already know. And it's the most amazing thing ever.'

Chouko peered at me. 'Whatever do you mean?'

I took a huge gulp. Was I really going to do this? I hoped the others were managing to slow the woman down. But it wouldn't take long to load the seedlings into the van. No. I had to do it, and I had to do it right now. And there was no time to get there slowly.

'Chouko, what if dragon-fruit trees really did grow dragons?'

She let out a little snort of laughter. But when I kept her gaze, her forehead wrinkled.

'Don't be silly, Tomas. I suppose next you'll be telling me crabs drop out of crab apples and fairies really do fly out of fairy cakes.'

'I'm serious,' I said. And Chouko must have thought it was all just a huge joke, because I broke into the biggest sunniest grin ever. But it wasn't because I'd suddenly found anything funny. It was because I could prove it.

'Turn around,' I said simply.

Chouko, still looking perplexed, slowly turned her head . . . and then slammed her hand over her mouth.

Because there, hovering just above us, was the glorious shining ruby shape of Flicker. And what's more, he wasn't alone! A slender dragon with four beautiful wings like a dragonfly was flying alongside him. I grinned as I recognised the dragon from Aura's pictures, the same one Elvi had drawn in her diary and told her stories about. Rosa's dragon! The dragon's four wings glittered and sparkled and its breath was a ripple of colour, just like a rainbow.

Chouko gasped and staggered back, her arm shooting out to shield me. But I laughed and ducked round her, rushing forward to wrap my arms around Flicker's scaly neck as he landed in Chouko's garden.

For a few minutes I thought she had gone into some kind of trance, that the shock had turned her into

a statue. But then she clapped her hands and erupted into wild giggly laughter, her eyes sparkling with delight.

'We have to go,' I said, and started pulling her by the arm. 'I'll explain everything later, I promise. But now we have to rescue the seedlings.'

She nodded, breaking into a run, her eyes fixed on the dragons who had risen back up into the air and were flying above us.

When we reached the offices I skidded to a halt.

Aura stared past me at the four-winged dragon.

'Tomas, that's Mamma's dragon,' she whispered. 'It's come back.'

I nodded. 'I think Flicker brought it.' I turned to the others. 'Have you managed to stall them?'

'A bit,' Ted called. 'The bee dragons kept them on their toes. I think they might have a bit of a sting on

232

them. The only trouble is, stinging makes them a bit dozy afterwards, and what with Zing already out for the count we've been relying on Rosebud. She couldn't keep up the farting though. Once the two of them recovered from their hysterics, they loaded up the seedlings they were carrying into that van. They've gone back in for more. But they've locked the van so we can't rescue them.'

'What are we going to do?' Liam said.

'Chouko's going to stop them,' I replied, pointing to her as she hurried away into the building.

'Did she . . . you know . . . see Flicker?' he asked.

I nodded quickly. 'I had to tell her. We need her help.'

I looked at Aura. The four-winged dragon had landed and it was reaching out its head towards her, its ruby eyes sparkling. She gazed up at it, a huge smile spreading across her face.

'I remember you,' she whispered. And then added softly, 'I just wish Mamma did too.'

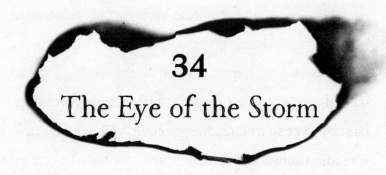

34
The Eye of the Storm

'Look, there's Chouko,' Ted said.

'It's no use,' she cried, hurrying towards us. 'They simply won't listen to me.'

'But we can't let them take the seedlings,' I pleaded. 'We're supposed to protect them!'

'We'd better think of something quick,' Liam said. And he pointed at the two figures carrying the last of the trays and placing them onto the trolley inside the van.

'I've got an idea,' Ted said. 'What if Zing zapped you into the van? Then maybe he could zap you *and* that trolley out of there.'

I looked around for Zing. He was still curled up in the grass. He raised his head sleepily.

'I think he used up all his charge getting me out of that building,' I said sadly. 'He'd need to be *super*-super-charged to do that.'

Ted looked thoughtful and then spun round to stare at Flicker. 'We have a storm dragon, remember? What if Zing met a bolt of lightning?'

'Er . . . he'd probably be a frazzled crisp,' I said.

'No,' Ted said. 'I don't think so. He doesn't react to electrical charge like we do. He feeds off it. It makes him powerful. This could work, Tomas.'

I really wasn't sure, but Flicker was already launching into the air. And with a jolt I realised that Zing was perched on the end of his tail.

Higher and higher they flew, Flicker circling in ever tighter loops, his scales flickering through every colour. And everything became still as the darkening sky grew purple. There was a deep rumble, and for a second I thought it had come from an immense dragon beyond

the trees. But then an almighty crack of lightning split the sky, followed by a louder burst of thunder. We watched as more jagged bolts of fierce white lightning struck again and again. Flicker stopped spinning and I could see Zing poised, wings outstretched. With one flick of his tail Flicker sent Zing flying, straight into the path of the lightning. When it hit him the sky turned electric blue.

And Zing vanished.

He reappeared a second later in front of us. Dazzling so brightly we had to shield our eyes.

'Are you sure about this, Tomas?' Aura said nervously. 'He might be OK eating electricity, but you're not a dragon.'

'Also, you're not going to be able to pick up that trolley with all those seedlings on your own,' Chouko said. 'But I can. You trusted me enough to ask for my help. Now let me help.'

The woman in the van had started the engine and was calling to her companion to hurry up and get in.

'I think she's right,' Ted said. 'We've only got one shot at this. Let her do it.'

'OK,' I said. Then I leaned closer to Chouko and whispered, 'It feels horrible but only for a bit.'

She nodded and squeezed my hand. 'Thank you for telling me the truth.'

'They're going!' Ted cried. And sure enough, as soon as the man's door closed the van jerked away.

Chouko held out her hands and Zing flew over to her. And in a blinding flash of light they were both gone.

'How long does it take to grab a trolley and zap out again?' Liam asked as the seconds ticked by. 'Zapping's meant to be fast, right?'

We kept our eyes fixed on the van as it drove away up the path towards the main gate.

'Come on, Zing,' I muttered. 'You can do it.'

The van juddered to a stop and the man hopped out. He tapped a key code and the gate swung open.

As he got back in, the woman started driving off before he'd even closed his door. The gate closed behind them. And just like that they were gone.

The seconds ticked past and no one spoke. I think we all felt the same. That we had failed the dragons.

I felt Flicker's warm breath wrapping around me as he bent his head down. But I couldn't bear to look into his diamond eyes. And what about poor Zing?

Next to Aura, the four-winged dragon shook its head and let out a smoky sigh.

And then suddenly a voice called out from somewhere behind us.

'A little help, please.'

We all turned, but the path was empty.

'I'm up here,' came the rather wobbly voice.

Turning our gaze upwards to the treetops, we finally spotted Chouko. She was balanced precariously on a branch, arms wrapped round the trolley, her back up against the trunk. And there was Zing, flaked out next to the seedlings.

We all whooped in relief and began dancing round delightedly, laughing and high-fiving. Then, realising that Chouko wasn't feeling quite so relieved at being stranded up a tree, I called, 'Don't worry, we'll get you down.'

Ted and I climbed onto Flicker's back and he flew us up to the branch, where between us we took the trolley from Chouko. I was just wondering if

241

she would be able to climb down now, when the four-winged dragon appeared beside us and stretched out its neck. With eyes wide, Chouko clambered on and was lowered to the ground.

We all stood and stared at the seedlings in their little pots. And then I noticed the cloud of bee dragons hovering nearby. They weren't dozy any longer, they were humming. As Aura held out a tub of cacao, one by one they broke formation and dived down to pick some up in their claws. We watched as they darted from seedling to seedling. Back and forth they went until they'd visited every single one. Then the little dragons rose into the air,

circled the seedlings and headed back towards Aura. Her face lit up as they settled on her, covering her arms and head with their jewel-like wings and flicking tails.

'I wish I could see their faces when they open up the van and find it empty,' Liam said, grinning.

'We really need somewhere safe to keep them though,' Chouko said. 'They've raised quite a few eyebrows while I've been caring for them. Dr Meadows may not be the only one to start taking an interest.'

'We've got the perfect place,' Aura said, beaming. 'I think it's time we took Chouko to your grandad's garden, don't you, Tomas?'

35
Time to Meet the Dragons

Crammed into Chouko's little car, trays of seedlings on our laps, we threaded our way through the streets, every so often catching glimpses of Flicker and the four-winged dragon as they soared across the moonlit sky.

'It'd be faster by dragon,' Aura whispered.

I grinned and imagined Flicker swooping down, gripping the roof of the car with his talons and lifting us up and away from the traffic.

By this time of the evening Grandad would usually be happily settled in his armchair, flicking through gardening magazines and pretending to stay awake through whatever TV show he and Nana were watching. But when we drew up and came round the side of the house I could see the light on in his shed. And there he was, standing outside, waving his hands at something, like he was shooing it away.

But it wasn't the two enormous dragons who had landed in his garden that were the problem. It was the twenty or so tiny shapes flitting around him.

He ducked and put his hands over his head as he spotted me.

'Hey, up, Chipstick. I'm glad you've turned up. We've got an excitable bunch on our hands this time.'

His eyebrows shot upwards when he saw Chouko, but a lime-green dragon zipped down and swiped at his head with its tail before he could say anything.

To her credit, Chouko took the garden of crazed dragons in her stride. 'Chouko Sato,' she said, hurrying over to give his hand a shake. 'Tomas has kindly offered to show me your incredible dragon-fruit tree.'

'Well, I think it's more their tree than ours,'

chuckled Grandad, pointing at the dragons. 'But let's see if we can send this lot on their way and then I can give you a proper tour.'

We ran around doing our best to shepherd them upwards, but these dragons were far more interested in playing games than leaving. It soon turned into a game for us too and we all ended up giggling and muddy.

Until, that is, Aura let out a wail.

'Oh no!' she cried. 'Look, it's Mamma and Papi.'

I spun round, and sure enough Aura's parents had appeared at the back door, with Nana. And they weren't the only ones. Mum, Dad and Lolli were there too.

'What are we going to do?' Aura hissed.

Rosebud, Zing and the flitter of tiny shapes zooming back and forth could be mistaken for birds or disappear into the darker corners. But right now we had Flicker and the four-winged dragon filling up most of the end of the garden. There was no way we could hide *them*. Especially not in the next twenty seconds. I watched our parents making their way up the garden path, Lolli skipping ahead, arms waving and not a toilet-roll bandage in sight.

'Any cunning plans?' Ted said. 'Hey, Liam, you got that hypno-magnet? We can dangle it in front of them.'

I looked all around and then back at Aura. There was more written on her face than just alarm and worry. As her eyes flitted between me and her dad, I could see glimmers of hope and excitement. I took a deep breath and then smiled at her.

'You know what? I don't think we need to hypnotise them. I think it's time they met the dragons.'

Aura beamed at me and immediately ran down the path towards her parents.

Mum and Dad raced over and wrapped me in a huge squeezy hug, and I saw Aura's family was doing the same. Just for a second I thought the grown-ups were all like Rosa and couldn't even see the dragons. But then I realised they were just relieved to see us safe.

It's weird how parents react to things. I mean, sometimes they completely lose their cool over the fact you've spilt a glass of milk on the living-room carpet, and other times you present them with a garden full of dragons and they just totally deal with it.

'I *knew* something was up, Tomas,' said Mum. 'But I have to admit, dragons weren't my first thought!' She looked around and laughed when she saw Dad with a dragon happily settled on his head, its tail swinging back and forth across his nose.

'I'm going to need a bigger jam tart to feed this lot,' Nana chuckled.

Lolli suddenly squeaked and pointed up to the sky. Little shiny tears cascaded down her cheeks.

'Tinkle!' she cried. And she skipped with joy as the silver-blue dragon circled the garden and flew down to her. She rushed over and flung her arms around the

248

dragon's scaly neck. 'Tinkle all better,' she murmured. And Tinkle replied with a soft sonorous song that swept across the garden.

36

Is It a Cuttlefish?
Is It an Onion?
No, It's a Dragon!

Over by the dragon-fruit tree Aura and her dad were peering at a fruit that had just burst and a tiny orange dragon with twisty horns and spiked tail still covered in seeds and sticky goo was peering back at them. Aura clapped her hands delightedly as the dragon hopped onto her dad's outstretched hand. But when he held it up to show Rosa, it was obvious she couldn't see what had made them both so excited. I watched Aura's face crumple.

Zing, who had regained his zinginess and completed another spinning somersault above me, hovered in midair, his eyes fixed on Aura. He darted towards Rosa, looped around her head and then disappeared in a flash of brilliant white. He reappeared across the garden, right in front of the four-winged dragon.

Obviously startled, it shook its head wildly and unfurled its wings, as if preparing to take off. But then we saw something happen. Its wings, which had been pink, started to pulse different colours.

'Hey!' Ted cried. 'Look at its wings – the way the colours are rippling! It's just like that cuttlefish Mr Firth showed us.'

Suddenly, right then, I had one of those moments where if I had scales they'd have been flaring bright gold. And it was thanks to Zing.

'That's why Rosa can't see the dragons!' I cried.

'What do you mean?' Liam asked.

'Remember Arturo's letter? He said Rosa was playing in the garden. But not just playing – she was leaping out at the dragons.'

'Er . . . yeah, so?' Liam said.

Ted's face had broken into a grin; he'd already worked it out.

'Think about it – when animals get startled, they defend themselves,' he explained. 'Just like Mr Firth said. Some curl up in a ball, some attack, some change colour to blend in. We've seen dragons with all sorts of special abilities.'

I jumped in. 'What if the dragon Rosa surprised had a very special way of defending itself,' I said. 'What if it could make you forget you'd seen it completely?'

'A hypno-dragon!' Liam cried.

'And Mamma frightened the dragon, didn't she?' said Aura. 'She was wearing a Halloween mask when she leaped out. So her dragon wouldn't have recognised her.'

'That's right!' I said. 'The dragon must have reacted by instinct. It was only a young one. It probably hadn't learned to control its powers yet, just like Zing when he started zapping.'

The dragon slowly moved towards Rosa. Folding back its wings, it stretched its neck out until its head was right in front of her. Then it stared at her. It looked sad and yet I could see it was as full of hope as we were. Clearly it hadn't meant to hypnotise Rosa all those years ago. For a second we all waited, holding our breath. But Rosa was too busy looking in every other direction and chattering away about this and that and nothing in particular. The dragon gave a rumbling sigh and made to turn away.

But then Grandad stepped forward. He ran a hand over the dragon's head.

'You know, Rosa, we grow all sorts of things in this garden,' he said. 'Cucumbers, tomatoes, runner beans.'

'How lovely,' Rosa said. 'My mamma would be delighted to know that you've kept the garden so well. Aura is very like her – she loves growing things.'

'She certainly does,' Grandad said, giving Aura a wink.

He reached down and picked out an onion from his wheelbarrow. Then held it up in front of Rosa.

Opposite her, the dragon leaned in and sniffed it.

'Sometimes we have to look a little bit harder,' Grandad said. 'Some people might just see a muddy onion. Someone else might see an interesting multi-layered vegetable that's been around for more than seven thousand years.'

He dug his thumb in and peeled it apart. 'But it has so many layers.' He paused, giving Rosa time to take it in, while the dragon waited, its eyes still fixed on her.

'For those one or two who really look, they might just see –' and as he quickly pulled the onion away, he whispered – '*a dragon*!'

Suddenly Rosa's eyes widened. She let out a squeak and stumbled backwards, landing on her bottom in the mud.

Aura rushed to help her up as Rosa stared straight ahead, her outstretched finger waggling at the dragon now craning its head down to her.

Onions make you cry when you cut them. Ted says it's a really complicated chemical process that creates this gas with a very long name, but right then I didn't think what was happening was the onion's fault.

'Do you remember?' Aura urged.

And Rosa, tears shining on her cheeks, looked deep into her eyes and nodded, a smile lighting up her face.

37
All That Possibility Just Waiting

Everything in Grandad's garden was blooming. In fact, thanks to his and Jim's efforts over the last few months – plus a little help from Rosebud! – the whole village was a blaze of colour. Bright yellows and pinks, reds and oranges tumbled from window boxes and hanging baskets everywhere, leading to the willow arch at the village centre. Here, flowers threaded their way through the branches, forming an intricate design, one that Grandad had definitely had a hand in. A poppy-and-cornflower dragon stretched its way up one side and, thanks to some sweet peas, it roared a rainbow of colour.

'I'm not sure everyone quite gets what it is,' Grandad had chuckled when he'd shown us.

'I think you have to be looking at it in the right way,' I replied. '*We* know it's there.'

His eyes twinkled. 'Those dragons of yours have certainly added a splash of colour to our little village, Tomas. In more ways than one.'

I'd been digging for hours in the garden when Grandad finally called me over, waving Nana's tin of goodies.

'She really wasn't joking about making a jam tart big enough for a dragon,' Grandad said. 'And it looks like she couldn't make up her mind about the flavour either.'

'It's a vast plate-sized jam tart,' I said, remembering the day I'd first found the dragon-fruit tree. 'With different-coloured sections like a multi-topping pizza. "Just think of the possibilities," you said.'

He laughed.

'Who'd have thought it, hey, Chipstick? All that possibility in our little garden.'

I looked over at Flicker stretched out under the apple trees, Zing happily perched in between his horns. And then at the dragon-fruit tree, and the vivid orange tendrils shooting out like bursts of flames. One night soon, there would be huge moon-white flowers. And then another crop of dragon fruit growing red and ripe. And bursting into life.

I grinned. Grandad licked the jam from his fingers.

'Come on then, show us that photo of Aura.'

We sat on the bench outside his shed and I pulled out the photo I'd printed out. It was of Aura and her parents in Mexico, outside a house that was painted bright orange. Next to them stood an old man with a neatly cropped beard and moustache. His eyes were twinkling just like Grandad's. They had found Arturo!

And every time I looked at his broadly smiling face I felt my heart beat hard and strong, like the beat of Flicker's wings.

'He never gave up,' I said. 'Arturo spent all those years looking for the dragons, hoping he might find the missing seed.'

'And now he's finally going to grow dragons,' Grandad said, leaning back.

'He always told Elvi that he wanted her to have one of the seeds so there would be hope in two places,' I added.

'And now you're doing the same by sending him one of the new seedlings.'

I smiled as my gaze rested on Arturo's open palm and the little pot sitting there, with its green shoot peeking out.

'The dragons need us all,' I said.

He rested a hand on my knee and smiled.

'You know, everything in this garden's growing so fast,' he said. 'Including you, Chipstick.'

We sat there for a few minutes, just us in our garden with one huge dragon and one tiny dragon. And a world of possibility, just waiting.

And then someone hollered and I looked up to see Ted and Liam racing down the path. And behind them came three more figures. In the middle was Lolli, skipping and giggling, and on either side were Kat and Kai, back for the holidays.

The superhero squad had grown too, and whether we were apart or close by we would always stick together, like the very best jam tarts, and we would always look after the dragons.

'Come on,' Kai called. 'We just saw Crystal and

Dodger flying over. The dragons are waiting for us in the Dragons' Den.'

'And we've got something we need to share,' said Kat excitedly. And as she reached me she thrust a photograph into my hand, her eyes gleaming.

So it turns out we were wrong – ours wasn't the only dragon-fruit tree growing dragons. And that means you should keep your eyes open and your oven gloves and water pistols handy. Because who knows, there could be dragons out there waiting for you too!

Acknowledgements

Luckily I've had five books to spread my thanks over. There have been a lot of people who have helped make this dream come true for me and it's been great to have the chance to mention them along the way.

I'll always be grateful to my lovely agent Jo Williamson and my fabulous editor Georgia Murray and the whole team at Piccadilly Press, for helping to bring my dragons into the world. And to Sara Ogilvie for creating artwork that is just so special and continually makes me smile. You're a roarsome lot! Sorry, but I had to get one dragon pun in before the series ended.

For me these books have always been about family, friendship and finding a little bit of magic in the everyday.

I can't thank my own family and friends enough for always cheering me on and providing such fertile soil to plunder. There's so much of my own parents in Tomas's nana and grandad. I've been lucky to be surrounded by kindness, teasing, comfort and love and I hope this has come through into the story and warms you as you read.

Thank you too to Isla and Esmé for inspiring so much of Lolli – you're a joy and we love you lots! (And sending thanks to your lovely mum and dad, Jo and Simon, for letting us borrow from you!)

And now to you, my dragon desperados. The readers who, by sitting down and curling up with the story, ignite the magic. Thank you for taking the dragons into your hearts. You are the best superhero squad ever!

And finally to Ian, Ben and Jonas, none of this would have happened without you. You are my true magic in the everyday. With you, I soar.

Keep dreaming of dragons, keep believing.